RICHARD MATHESON
UNCOLLECTED

Backteria and Other Improbable Tales

RICHARD MATHESON
UNCOLLECTED

Backteria and Other Improbable Tales

GAUNTLET PRESS

■ 2012 ■

Manufactured in the United States of America

Gauntlet Publications
5307 Arroyo Street
Colorado Springs, CO 80922
(719) 591-5566
www.gauntletpress.com
info@gauntletpress.com

To Henry Kutner—
with thanks for his encouragement.

—RM

Table of Contents

Backteria

My name is Emery Wilson, PhD. I work for *The Svennington Laboratory*. What we do is locate, isolate and investigate exotic viruses and bacteria. Such as MY-7, a virus which causes night sweats, cramps and loss of memory. A portion of this extends unhappily to loss of identity.

In the unhappy case of Arthur Bland this identity loss grew so severe that he not only forgot who he was but what he was. This resulted in a total lapse of human traits. Mr. Bland became convinced that he had become simian and insisted on living in a tree, sustaining his bodily well-being on a diet of bananas and leaves. This condition persisted until, during sleep one night, he fell from the tree and broke his neck, dying instantly. The autopsy revealed no more than the presence of MY-7 in his system.

But that is not my account so I will not dwell on it. All I intended to transmit was the information regarding my profession. Such as the investigation of such bacteria as X9-1, which caused such an excessive loss of balance that most victims of its invasion kept falling on their heads, which resulted in a noticeable percentage of concussions. But, that too, is a different story albeit a sad one. What I mean to tell you is another one. A grim and dreadful one.

~~~~~~~~~~~~~

Stanley Barenbaum, M.D. was rotund and worried. The rotund part was easy to see, visible to the eye. The worried part was more difficult. I had to surmise it. I was able to do this. Dr. Barenbaum had the expression of a man married to a sex-obsessed woman who, arriving home early one afternoon, sees his handsome brother-in-law's red BMW convertible parked in the driveway of his home. Definitely apprehensive.

"Good afternoon," he muttered.

I waved him to the chair opposite my desk. He sat down, tentatively, I thought, as though he was prepared to leap to his feet at a moments notice. His smile looked frozen to me.

"What can I do for you?" I asked.

He didn't answer at first but drew in a deep draught of air through his nose. Then he said, "This virus. If that's what it is. We aren't certain what it is. We only know it exists. No, we don't even know that for sure. We only know what we *think* it is and we're not even certain of that. But we *do* believe it exists and we're anxious to know—"

At which point he ran out of breath and was compelled to inhale, wheezingly.

"You have a specimen with you?" I asked, speaking quickly lest he interrupt me with another rant.

"We sent it in several days ago," he said, now sounding almost like a rational human being.

"I haven't seen it yet, I'm sorry," I apologized. "I'll get to it as soon as possible. Have any of my associates given your office an analysis yet?"

"*No*," said Dr. Barenbaum. Whether in irritation or despair—or both—I couldn't tell. Part was certainly despair. "We *must* ascertain what it is," he said. Definitely despair.

"What is it about this virus—if, indeed, it *is* a virus—that concerns you so?" I inquired.

He didn't answer. I sensed that he was loathe to do so.

"Doctor?" I said.

I hadn't taken notice of his Adam's apple. I did now as it dipped abruptly and the sound of his nervous swallow was clearly audible. "Please," I said. By now my curiosity was piqued.

"We refer to it as *VD-1*," he said in a muffled voice.

"I beg your pardon?" I responded; not sure I'd heard him correctly.

"*VD-1*," he told me again.

"Oh," I hesitated, then added, "Does that—stand for anything?"

"It *does*," he said. His voice was now thin and strengthless.

"Which is?" I had to prompt him.

He sucked in air.

"*Virtual Disappearance*," he said.

~~~~~~~~~~~~

Dead silence in my office. Was the man serious? Or was I the butt of some inner-office prank? How could I tell?

I decided to pursue the matter. Barenbaum *was* a doctor wasn't he? He seemed sincere enough. No point in dismissing the situation pro bonum. My mind doesn't work that way.

His rumination changed my mind in the silence.

"I know this sounds improbable," said Dr. Barenbaum. (I chose to leave his title unchallenged for the moment.)

"Let me understand this," I said, "You refer to disappearance. Do you mean that literally?"

"I do," said Barenbaum.

"In what way?" I asked, I winced at the notion. "The dissolving of organs? Partial or total dissolution?"

"No," he said.

"All right," I went on. "What *were* the symptoms then? Sweats, dizziness, drowsiness, diarrhea, *what*?"

"No," he said.

"For God's sake, Dr. Barenbaum," I protested, "What were the symptoms?"

"I told you." Now he sounded impatient.

"You said—" I began.

"I said disappearance," he interrupted, "I mean total, absolute, complete *disappearance*."

"Let me get this straight," I said. "You're saying—!"

"Oh, for heaven's sake!" He was furious now. "Don't you comprehend English? Israel Kenshaw disappeared! Physically! Absolutely! In *toto*!"

I comprehend English. I could not comprehend what he was talking about.

"How did this occur?" I inquired. Quietly. Devoid of rancor. My way.

"He went in the bathroom," said Dr. Barenbaum. He actually gulped. "And vanished."

"You mean—?" I started.

"I mean he *vanished*!" raged Dr. Barenbaum. "The bathroom door was opened after a while and he was gone! *Disappeared*!"

Backteria

I couldn't accept his account: Not yet. There had to be some logic to it.

"What about the window?" I queried. Surely that was an explanation.

"*It was locked*," he answered. He was getting tired of speaking to me now. "Anyway, it was too small. Mr. Kenshaw was, to be blunt, obese."

He leaned forward in the chair and spoke slowly and distinctly. For the last time, I sensed. "Mr. Kenshaw—"

"Your patient," I said.

"My *patient*." His voice was tight, almost threatening. "He went into the bathroom on the evening of the twenty-fifth…"

"The twenty-fifth," I repeated.

"*Yes*," he said through clenched teeth. "He went in with a smile on his face."

Ah, I thought. A smile. Was that significant? I didn't see how it could be but I was grasping at straws. How could we be talking about a virus now? Or for that matter, a bacteria?

"I didn't hear the rest of that, " I said. I hadn't. "Would you repeat—?"

"I *said*," he declared, " —that Mr. Kenshaw had entered the bathroom—"

"With a smile on his face," I amended.

"Yes!" he cried, "Which is hardly the point!"

"Which *is*—?" I probed. I felt a need to challenge his account.

"Which *is*," he held on. "Mr. Kenshaw went into the bathroom—*with a smile on his face*—" he added tensely, "He locked the door. His wife *heard* him lock the door."

"Go on," I said.

He shuddered. With aggravation I believe. "An hour later, his wife, receiving no reply to her questions, had the door unlocked. *Mr. Kenshaw was not in the bathroom. The bathroom was empty*."

"And—?" I asked.

"*And*?" he demanded.

I was really grasping at straws by then. "Was there by any chance—" I suggested totally straw grasping now. "—any…well—*ashes* on the floor?" It was the only thing I could come up with as farfetched as it was. Spontaneous Combustion. I'd read about it. Somewhere.

"*What*?" Barenbaum snapped.

"No…smell of burning flesh in the air?" I asked.

Teeth gritted again. He shook his head slowly. Very slowly.

"And you—believe that—*all this*—" I didn't know how else to put it. "Had some connection to the virus? The bacteria? whatever?"

"*I do*," he said. "What else—?"

"You know, for a fact, that *he'd* been infected?" I broke in.

"Of *course* I know! All my colleagues know! The blood test confirmed it!"

"I see," I nodded. Haplessly. "And you don't think—" I broke off. I'd been about to ask him if he thought Mr. Kenshaw's smile had anything to do with—no. That was ridiculous.

"Well, it only remains for us to examine the specimen," I told him. "See if there are any answers there."

"I would hope so," said Barenbaum stiffly.

"One more question," I said. "Did Mr. Kenshaw display any peculiarities of behavior prior to his—" Disappearance, I thought. I hadn't the heart to say it aloud.

"No, nothing," Barenbaum answered.

"Nothing at all?" I probed. "It might be evidential."

"*Nothing*," he emphasized. "The usual."

"Such as—?" I re-probed. Wondering, to myself, why I didn't just let go of the whole thing and concentrate on examination of the submitted specimen. Sure—

"His job, his health, his childhood, his car—"

Backteria

"His childhood," I thought. "Anything there?" I asked.

"*No*," he said. "Now will you—?"

"Immediately," I cut him off. "We'll start the examination right away."

~~~~~~~~~~~~

And start it we did. And discovered nothing pertinent. Unless establishing that it was definitely a bacteria bore any significance. We suspected that before we began the examination.

But VD-1? Not scientifically acceptable a label. How were we supposed to identify it? *The Smiling Germ*? Suggested one of our jokester assistants. *The Vanishing Cream*? *The Houdini Effecter*? Each suggestion was more absurd then the previous one. Accordingly, we merely assigned it the name BU-1. Bacteria Unknown—one.

Only one oddity emerged during the course of our study. One afternoon a thunderstorm caused a twenty minute discontinuation of our electric service. Much to our amazement, the bacteria sample on our electroscope glowed for a number of seconds, then disappeared from view. When the electricity was renewed, the electroscope plate was blank.

~~~~~~~~~~~~

By a distressing turn of events, BU-1, as we called it, began to spread in an alarming fashion, very soon taking on the threat of, first, an epidemic, then a pandemic. Newspaper and magazines were inundated with articles about the dire situation, most of them filled with conjecturing—most of it ridiculous—as to the possible meaning of the disappearance aspect.

One particularly mystifying element to the entire enigma was the remarkable fact that many of the BU-1 victims—approximately thirty-five percent did not disappear at all but suffered a few days of elevated temperature and, on occasion, a minor attack of mental disorientation before eliminating the bacteria from their system.

The remaining sixty-five percent vanished without a trace.

Explanations failed to elucidate, in any way, the uncanny vanishments. (An ungrammatical labeling of the vanishings by the press.)

~~~~~~~~~~~~

The answer—such as it was—came to my attention, seven weeks from the outset of *The Goodbye Plague* as it was now called. This in the guise of Colonel Ula Vanderloop. Commandant of *The Royal Dutch Retreat Corps*. Colonel Vanderloop, in addition to his military status was a well-known medium and faith healer, having achieved his spiritual eminence mainly through his well-known psychic communications with Jack the Ripper who denied all culpability with the White Chapel atrocities, claiming that on all those occasions he was attending Christian Science lectures in Dover.

Herewith, the details of my meeting with said Colonel Vanderloop. take it or leave it.

"Doctor Wilson," he began in a stentorian voice. Actually, he referred to me as "Docta Vilson" but we'll let that go. Any attempt to literalize his speech would be counter-productive.

He introduced himself as per my words, presenting his varied qualifications, both military and spiritual, in a high resonant manner.

Backteria

I waited for some cessation in his discourse, then asked him, politely of course, the reason for his visit. I wanted to ask why he was intruding on my busy afternoon but, again, politesse prevailed.

At which, the Colonel imparted to me the reason for his visit. An impartation (if there is such a word; if not, there should be) which gave me a literal shock. To be truthful, it jolted me in my chair.

"I have been in contact with Mr. Israel Kenshaw," was what he told me.

"You have—" I muttered incompletely. It was all I could say.

"—been in contact with him, yes," the Colonel completed. "You know about the man?"

My lips stirred without sound. Then I managed, "I do."

"For how long?" he asked.

"Long?" I said. I mumbled. "I never knew the man at all, only *about* him from Dr. Barenbaum."

"What I mean," continued Vanderloop, "what period of time were you acquainted with this man before he passed?"

"Passed," I said. Sounding like a numbskull kindergartener. I felt like one.

Obviously, the Colonel's regard for me was equally low. "Yes, *passes*," he said. "Passed on." He waited for some sign of comprehension in my face. Not forthcoming. His porcine features stiffened. "*Died*," he stated, obviously using a word anathema to him.

My mouth positively fell open. "I didn't know he had," I told him. This was casting an entirely new light on the BU-1 mystery. The first evidence of fatality.

Now Vanderloop's look became one of amusement. "How droll," he said. "Your Mr. Kenshaw was of an equal mind."

"Sir?" I asked.

"He insisted that he didn't know either."

"Know?" I said.

"*That he'd passed on, man!*" The Colonel cried.

"What did he *think* happened to him?" I asked. I really wondered.

Vanderloop sighed audibly. I could sense that he was not accustomed to this variety of Q and A exchange. He was the sort of man who was used to holding forth, to explaining measuredly, in a word, pontificating.

No point in my noting the bulk of our lengthy conversation. It went in circles, frustrating both of us.

What finally did become established was that we had no idea whatever about the spiritual status of Israel Kenshaw. Was he a surviving disincarnate communicating with the living? Or was he living himself, intent on explaining what had ensued following his unforeseen disappearance?

According to Kenshaw, he had traveled back in time to the year when he was ten years old, a particularly rewarding time of his life. His father was a forest ranger in Sequoia National Park and Kenshaw had been his dedicated "helper." The home he lived in was forest enclosed. He was an only child. He had never been more content.

Imagine his reaction then when, infected by BU-1, he vanished from his bathroom and found himself returned to that idyllic period of his childhood. Naturally there was the complication of his ten-year-old duplicate and his parents.

Understandable consternation. But these drawbacks seemed of little import to Kenshaw. He seemed overwhelmed with joy, asked to be remembered to Bianca, his wife of nine years and his few friends, extending his wish that they, too, become infected with BU-1 and return to some longed-for time of their lives.

I must add that all this information—coming especially from the lips of Colonel Ulu Vanderloop—took me off balance and made me more than dubious. For instance, if Kenshaw's back in 1956 how in the name of all that's holy, could he be contacting Vanderloop—and, of course, me—in 2011? His explanation that time is *flexible* failed to convince me.

Still, that it was Kenshaw was undeniable. As were the undeniable identities of so many other BU-1 victims whose account all bore the same points. *One*—that they *were* infected. *Two*—that they had disappeared—once almost fatally, as she was driving to work. *Thrice*—they had returned in time to happily recalled periods of their lives. *Four*—that they were very much enjoying their return in time.

In some cases, it was not to childhood. One elderly man "chose" (one assumes that choice was involved in all these peculiar transpositions) to return to the year he was Captain of a Navy Minesweeper in World War Two. Another aging beldame returned to the days when she was a chorus girl in a long-running Broadway Musical. And many more. The effect was state and worldwide. Consider the case of Bjorn Lutefisk who chose to return to his Uncle Olaf's herring factory as the floor manager. Unhappily, the smell reduced Mr. Lutefisk to a gibbering segment of his former self. Consequently, he ended up in an asylum. Uncle Olaf began to drink again since he had to contend with two versions of his nephew.

Strangely enough—or, perhaps understandably—a number of BU-1 victims went nowhere. They suffered their mild temperature elevation for a few days and, on occasion, a limited period of mental disorientation. From this, one is drawn to the conclusion that either the infection was not severe enough, or the victim involved had no particular spot in the past they yearned for.

None of which convinced me especially. Notably, the idea of time being flexible. Perhaps so but I was from Missouri on that point. Still, the evidence was there, irrefutable in every detail.

The ongoing and increasing – enigma was not clarified when some media wag in a *National Enquirer* type article defined it as the PUZZLE OF BACKTERIA. Ignoring the facts of the "puzzle," he claimed that all its victims went back to a time to a more genial environment. That this was not statistically accurate was shunted aside. So *Bacteria Unknown-1* became, permanently labeled as BACKTERIA.

~~~~~~~~~~~~

Not being a professional historian, I will make no attempt to enlarge on the subject. Suffice to say that the number of Backteria victims increased in the hundreds then, in a matter of months, to the thousands and, ultimately ten thousands. The increase, in other words, was geometric. This over the scope of every continent and island in the known world, including the Arctic zones. Not that every victim, as indicated, vanished. Many of them did however, a few of them "reporting in" — as one journalist expressed it — "via the medium of mediums."

Why this method was utilized was probably self-evident. There was, simply put, no other means of communication available, as obscure as the method proved to be. There was no other way to let those "left behind" know where their vanishing relatives or friends had gone. Especially perplexed by the process — although perfectly willing to "cash in" on it, was the multiple array of mediums throughout the world. Vanderloop alone became so well-to-do that he made a formal bid to purchase Holland in whole or in parts. I will not enumerate the many other mediums who acquired wealth through their intercessions. Most of them never really knew whether their "communications" were alive or dead. Not that it mattered to them.

Backteria

~~~~~~~~~~~~~

The most uniquely peculiar occurrence in this *Panoply of Plaguaries*, as they came to be called, was the incident of Dimitri R. Mupphinsky of Vladivostok. (Middle name Raga) His medium (name unintelligible) reported that Comrade Mupphinsky vanished from his place of business at the end of March. When he communicated with his Uncle Vanya in June, it was to state that he had gone back to his fathers' farm only to discover that his memory had erred and that life there was intolerable. Which established the conundrum that memory was, perhaps, fragile and not essentially reliable. However, if this "Backfire," as it came to be known, was in effect in other plague victims, I never found out.

~~~~~~~~~~~~~

My ill-advised participation in the Backteria Mystery took place approximately thirteen months following inception. By then, the disease (we felt obliged to term it so) was widespread. Every country on the globe suffered its share of the bizarre affliction. *The Svennington Laboratory* was deluged with involvement. That we had no more explanation for the dilemma than any other source didn't seem to matter. We were the first to be engaged in the "Vanishing Chaos" as it also came to be called and that was enough.

My own enmeshment was typical. My marriage was faltering. I felt scant attachment to Brenda and her regard for me was similar. The two girls were on their own, both married, with girls of their own. Work at the lab was increasingly unrewarding—especially as any attempt to achieve technological BU-1 explanation was invalid.

It was at that frustrating point that I made my decision.

It was simple to acquire a sample of BU-1. I had made up my mind not to take the haphazard course of seeing if I could "catch" the Backteria since it was easily available to me.

The main problem was to ascertain what period of my life I most aspired to. It never even occurred to me that I might be one of those infected victims who would not disappear but only be exposed to a few days of elevated temperature and perhaps, a brief period of mental disorientation. Far from it. I went all the way.

There was not a plentiful collection of choices to be made. My childhood was a possibility. Mother was a good-natured soul. Father drank some, but by and large was a passable sire. But nothing outstanding. My teenage years were unacceptable. An unhappy array of failed female liaisons and repetitive skin disorders.

My best bet, I decided at length, was the year 1950, Webster College, Miriam Gilford and, vividly in recollection, Professor Andrew Vaughn and Egyptology. With what graphic verbiage that man described the search for various Royal tombs such as Tutankhamen's.

Which is what brought me to this unpleasant situation, you see. How could I have known that my subconscious was so imbued with Andrew Vaughn's coercive descriptions that they filled my mind to the spilling point. For here I am in Egypt in the year 1922. No way of letting Brenda know my plight. Vanderloop is beyond my reach; that is for certain.

So who am I residing with? Mr. Howard Carter, as cranky and demanding a man as I have ever run across. Each day in *his* tomb—he will permit no credit otherwise—is a lasting travail. I made the blunder of commenting on his feeling for Lord Carnavon's daughter—which comment displeased him greatly. The fact that I know he never will consummate his lingering desire for her only makes my state of mind more untenable. My only consolation is the fact that I will not be confronted by my younger self. But *damn* it's hot! I mean *hot*!

He Wanted to Live

And in the early morning when he had just about managed to fall into a troubled sleep—Lucy woke him up.

He was all curled up like a fetus in one corner of their bed. He jumped when she touched him. He jumped as if he'd been stabbed. He stared at her in terror. He wanted to shout at her—Don't you dare come near me! She was used to his nerves and she didn't know it was more than nerves now. She said—Breakfast—and she went out of the bedroom.

He lay back on the pillow and looked at the ceiling with hopeless resignation. He looked until his heart slowed down and his hands stopped shaking. He looked out of the window at the gray silence of another morning. Another day. Another collection of wracking hours.

The process began. His brain had hardly dragged itself from darkness. But it started to leave him. He couldn't control it. It thought everything he didn't want it to think.

There was the ceiling and there were the walls. Look at that crack in the ceiling. Suppose the roof gave. Suppose the attic with its dusty forgotten contents showered down on him. Suppose he were crushed as he lay there, the stored away relics breaking every bone.

Maybe the house would catch fire. Lucy was in the kitchen. She gets careless. A flame shoots out from the stove. Ignition. Conflagration.

He dressed and he was afraid. He might catch a germ from the clothes. The tie, the shirt, the coat might get caught in some machinery somewhere—who knew where. It might twist his flesh and cut off his breath, make his veins and arteries stand out in stark relief like pulsing tubes of blue spaghetti. His shoes might force a nail to grow back in. There might be poisoning in his system, blood rotting at the edges and flowing deep in congested waves.

He washed carefully and, when he shaved, his hand shook for fear he would cut his throat. He'd meant to get an electric razor. Why did he always forget? He looked in the cabinet. It was full of death. An unwary opening of bottles, a swallow and quick finish. He slammed the cabinet door shut and hurried out of the bathroom.

He descended slowly on the stairs so he wouldn't fall and shatter his body at the foot of the steps. His house was a trap, a snare set by himself and all the men and women who made it what it was. Shifting rugs and loose connections. Smooth floor and smoother bathtubs, burning radiators and fireplaces and furnaces. Broken glass and razor blades and splinters and sharp knives. Man built himself a home and filled it with menace. It was all right when you didn't think about it. But then something happened and you thought about it all the time.

He Wanted to Live

At breakfast he wondered if maybe Lucy was poisoning him. She loved him. He knew that. She had married him and borne him two fine children. But maybe she was poisoning him. Maybe there was poison in the orange juice, sprinkled in with the salt and pepper and the sugar. Maybe he was packing death into his veins shouting—Here! Run riot in my blood!

He shuddered when she brushed against him. He was afraid for the children. And he was afraid of the children. They were his. He loved them with all his heart. He was afraid of them. Breakfast and supper on weekdays were agonies of wretched ambivalence. It got so he hated everyone at some time or another.

The subway station was very crowded. There were people lined up at the edge of the platform. The train whistled far away. They all shifted on their feet and moved closer to the edge. They touched him, pushed him, shoved him. He wanted to scream. They were trying to push him over the edge.

Suppose they did. Suppose the great steel mass slammed into him and crushed him to a pulp on the track, severed his limbs from his body, sent sprays of his blood into the air, splattered his organs on the black ties, coated the pillars with his flesh.

He wanted to yell, to strike out blindly, to fight for his life. But he was civilized. He was a modern. He was a man. He couldn't cry or shriek. He had to pretend he wasn't afraid. He must make believe he was used to this—the surrounding of death in life.

The train was crowded. It was always crowded in the morning. The sweat trickled down his face and across his neck and down from his armpits. The people were packed against him. Packed people were death. Alone they were bad enough. In a mass, in a swaying dimlit mass, they were death itself. They mingled with each other, each of them joined with another and, all added up, they were crawling twisting death, all around him. Calling him, plucking at his clothes with flesh-tattered skeleton fingers.

He wondered if he should get off and take the local because there were always less people on the local.

But it was figuring like that that killed a man. Suppose he got on the local in order to avoid the crowds on the express. That day the local would have an accident. He knew it would. That was the way.

Then again, the local went under the river and the express went over it. If he was going to face death then he would rather it was on the express than on the local. Because it would be better to fall off the bridge. There might be a chance—just an outside chance—that he would get to a window and maybe swim up to the surface. He could see the light anyway. It would be better to see the light.

If there was an accident under the river he couldn't see anything. It would be pitch black. If the tunnel walls collapsed and the water rushed in, he'd be drowned in muddy torrential darkness. It would be dark because the electricity would short circuit. There would be people electrocuted and screaming and in the dark he could smell their flesh burning. He couldn't stand that. Water rushing up, up swimming over him, screams in the blackness and drowning. Floating corpses in the black tunnel filled with water. It would be better to go the other way.

He took the express. And the people pushed against him and the train got more crowded at every station. He couldn't bear to be touched by the people. He shrank away from them and tried to stand apart. How did he know that some of them didn't have awful diseases and if they touched him he might get the disease too? Heat made germs float around in the air. Invisible little bugs floating on coughs and everybody's breath.

He Wanted to Live

He had to get away. There had to be somewhere. Everywhere he went there was death and he was afraid. He wanted to live. But death was everywhere. He couldn't get away from it.

At the office, he shivered at his desk. Suppose the building caught on fire and he was trapped. The flames roaring around and blisters and reddening skin and burning alive, horror-stricken screams. He couldn't bear such agony.

Suppose the building collapsed. He'd hear of such things happening. After all, he was placing his life in the hands of an architect and engineers and builders and how did he know they were trustworthy? How did he know some engineer wasn't mad at something and he didn't make the right figures and seams cracked and the building caved in. The huge beams would crush him. He'd be hurtled to the sidewalk. His head would pop on the concrete like an egg and his brains would spill all over the sidewalk.

He thought about these things all the time. He couldn't work. He sat and scribbled on pieces of paper and thought about dying. How could a man concentrate when he was always fearing? He wanted to live but he couldn't see how. Everything was against him. There weren't any percentages. Everywhere he went, death was waiting for him. He had nothing to say about it. It was going to happen and maybe in the next second. He couldn't alter it. All he could do was think and wonder about it and drive himself sick with worrying.

At lunch he thought that the waiter and the cook in the restaurant were conspiring to poison him. He couldn't eat the food. It choked in his throat. He ate little bits of it to see if he could taste any poison. He tried to dilute it with water.

Then he broke out into a cold sweat because it occurred to him that the water might be poisoned too. So he made the waiter bring him some water from the next table. He knew he was a fool for trying to trick the waiter. But he had to do it anyway.

All afternoon he wanted to scream and leap up from his desk and crash through the window. But he was afraid. He couldn't jump. He couldn't cry out—For God's sake, leave me be! He sat at his desk and shook with palsied terror. His brain teemed with thoughts of the many ways a man can die each day. Each was more terrible than the one before. Each heaped its horror on the next until, after a while, he was no better than a helpless child whimpering in the night, fearing each sudden sound and movement. He hungered for peace and there was no peace. Terror was his only food.

When work ended at five, he had to go back to the subway. By that time he was gutted with horror and he stood dull-eyed and limp and was too weak to even shudder. Once more he went through the whole train of thought about the local and the express. It was like a separate litany in his brain. He couldn't stop it any more than he could voluntarily stop breathing.

At home he found the same threats waiting for him. He unlocked the door and stepped into the trap he had formed around him. He ate supper, hating and distrusting his wife and his children and even himself. Fear surrounded him like a shifting mist.

He was afraid of the house. He was more afraid to leave it. Lucy complained. But he wouldn't go anywhere. He sat in his chair quietly and clung to the arms and tried to keep from screaming. Then his mind began to pick out sounds and he began to feel death walking in his house, watching and waiting for him to make one slip, one incautious move.

He wanted to live!

He Wanted to Live

He wanted to live in peace and quiet but they wouldn't let him.

He went to bed early because there was no comfort in waking.

He tossed and turned alone. Lucy would not go to bed so early.

She stayed downstairs and read.

He tried to think of nothing. But his mind would not blank itself. It went on and on. The roof was cracking, the floor was giving, the house was on fire, his system ran with poison, he was sick with infesting germs, there was a prowler with a gun, there was a mad dog outside the door, Lucy was sneaking up the stairs with a butcher knife.

He turned and screamed into the pillow so no one could hear his madness ringing out in the night.

Later he drifted away.

He dreamed the same dream over and over. The falling object, the ugly mushroom of billowing smoke, the spray of burning fire. He writhed with agony as it covered him. There were people watching. Lucy—he screamed—Lucy kill me, please kill me. I can't bear the pain. Please, please kill me.

She laughed at him. His children laughed. Everyone passed him by and laughed.

He was in torture. His body flared up. It was a white hot coal. He screamed from the pain. But they made him live. Live, live!—they cried. It was a chant in the night, a taunt from the blackness of dreaming. Death would not come then and take away the pain. It stood and watched but it would not come close. Live, live!—it laughed out loud.

He cried, he screamed and woke up to find himself sitting in bed and staring at the night.

The same nightmare?—said Lucy.

29

Yes—he said.

He sat up for an hour. Then he fell back in a stupor of weariness. He closed his eyes and prayed for a dreamless rest.

And in the early morning when he had just about managed to fall into a troubled sleep—Lucy woke him up.

Life Size

The littler one was playing with her dollhouse this afternoon. Crinkled knees on rose bespattered rug, she fondled her ones, Molly, Fig and the Puppy Gruff.

Molly is a boy doll. The littler one giggled when I dubbed him so. That is a girl's name, she said. Hush, said I, who is to say?

Fig is a black sambo rajah, jeweled and awesome. And the Puppy Gruff is the Puppy Gruff.

Mother was sitting at the big furniture scraping on a hill of debts.

She frowned at me squatting on a buttoned hassock admiring my daughter.

The littler one was rearranging furniture, a blue-veined hand sliding a bathtub to the wall. You must not place a bathtub in the guestroom, I told her, the guests might float ducks in it. I flew a bit of breeze from my lips and the delicate hair wisps at her temple stirred golden. Pap*pa*, said she with a shake.

The furniture arrangement proved so distasteful that she swept her hand across the floor to brush it clean. The furniture bounced nicely on the rug. I think now, said I, that is some fine way to arrange furniture. Little lips pouting, priceless petulance. The distaff giant rose, the floor shook with her coming. I looked up and the far off eyes sprinkled ice dust on our heads.

Get up! she cried. I lifted the piano with two fingers. First, I begged, we must return this.

She bent over and slapped it spinning on the floor. Come here, in a loud way she said. And *you*, a finger spear pointing at my loved one's heart, stay away from the house if you don't appreciate it.

Little head lowered, rising tears. You may play nicely with the house, I said and stood up way high. Mother stamp stamped to the table. I stamp stamped followed.

This simply cannot go on, she gurgled, pushing the everest of bills to me. I am not hungry, I said. Ice dust upon me.

Listen Peg, she hissed so the littler one would hear worse, this simply is the end. Either you get out and work or I leave, *with* the child.

Old tale. Old song. Old misery set to words. Take *my* child? Nonsense.

I'll get work tomorrow, I promised.

Tomorrow, tomorrow I heard an echo from the valley of her throat. How many times have I heard that? How many times did Sal hear it? Tomorrow I said and walked away. That is not all, she cried but I kept on for the doorway.

It is unbelievable the rapidity with which I shrank. Suddenly from as big as her, down, down.

Life Size

Whishhh, the doorway far far up like a mountain tunnel. The huge chair noted and prepared to collapse its gargantuan crimson on my tiny body. The sky shook, the cliff tottered miles above me,

I flung up my arm and cried fear.

Pain at my knees. Suddenly I was back again, sprawled across the chair. Pappa! Sweet worried tones caressed my ears.

Mother had such a look and such a trembling, standing by the table choking herself.

I rose with dignity and brushed off some dust not on me. I strode into the hall carefully. The house was slowly beginning to rock. The stairs were swelling, receding, in and out, like rolling wave carpeted and tacked.

I held tight to the banister. No sense being swept out the window and so to sea.

I prisoned off my room and sat down uh! on my white bed. My feet raised up and placed *so* on the spread, I fell back.

The pitching slacked off, my ship slid into calm waters. Oh Sal, I whispered, Sal who understood, Sal not here, Sal far away gone and never coming more.

The clock whispered sleep and wake.

I rose squarely up and was without trouble. The room, the hall, all in fine order, walls square, flat and firm, steady ceiling.

I slid down the silent stairs. Ha ha was the chuckle as I swept past the bottom toe and kneeled before the living room. Murmurs in the kitchen, the way clear. Softly, softly. Hello there Fig old bedizened potentate. Molly.

I began to crawl carefully, slowly.

For a while, naturally, I got nowhere since I kept shrinking the farther I went. The room swelled bigger, bigger. Grotesque universe.

Voices! Footsteps!

I scurried to the brink of the rug meaning to slip quickly over the edge and crouch in a hairy black cavern.

Peg! Voice in the distance, crashing from the sky. I could have sworn I was out of sight.

Peg! The thunder roared again.

I wept with fury biting at the roses for their eyes so keen. I raised a look through binocular tears.

The little one, clever darling, made as though frightened. Sweet conspirator! Mother will not know my plan from her.

I started climbing up the red chair, a long haul without a rope.

Fantastic hands reached down to smother me in hot greasy palms. I clawed at them, angular sweating monstrosities.

The room wavered, so like it to do that.

I stood up, ready to die for my secret, let the black waves dash on me. The room distorted, cooled and shrank. I held up my hands, screaming, ready for the ceiling to plunge down on me.

But first the tower of me crashed an awful way far down on the rug plateau. I saw roses in my eye when I became unknowing.

I woke in my bed feeling quiet. Someone was sitting across the room.

Come here Sal, I asked so gently. Let me touch your cold gray lips, let me see the clay that stains your eyes.

It was only a white tower that came to me as I slowly drowned in the lake folds of my bed.

Foul lifeguard it reached down and tugged me out. My wrist was enveloped by cold serpents. I heard hmmm at the tower gate. I squinted and saw it was actually a giant whose every pore was a gaping pit.

I turned my head away and was sick it was so ugly and horrible.

I fell away to black things soon.

Life Size

But before it, I thought this and final too.

When that bleak tower is gone or at slumber, I will creep out, fly down the steps of mountain side and run across the rose strewn plain to my home.

In the door, they will leave it open for me. Up, up, up the pretty stairs, two at a time I think.

Into the bed creeping to hear them whisper below, my friends.

Waiting for Sal to tuck me in and kiss me so, *goodnight dear.* Sleep.

Dream on dream within the smooth and creamy silent walls.

The pendulum stops.

Man with a Club

Jeez, wait'll I tell you what happened last night, Mack.
I swear you'll never believe it. You'll think I'm nuts.
But I swear Mack, I swear I seen it with my own
eyes.

I was out with Dot. *You* know, the broad that lives
down near Prospict Park. Yeah, you remember her.

Well, we was going up the Paramount t'see Frankie
Laine. Sat'day night, you know. Puttin' on the dog. Show,
feed, take her home, give'er the old one two.

Well, anyway, I guess it was, oh, seven thirty when
we come up from the I.R.T. station. Forty secon' street.
Time Square. You know the place. Where they got stores
down the stairs. They sell jelly apples and stuff. Yeah,
yeah, that's right.

So we come up the street, see? It's jus' like any time.
You know, all the t'eatres lit up, people walkin' around. I
grab Dot's arm and we head for Broadway.

Then I see a bunch o' guys across the street. So I figure it's probably some drunk cuttin' up. *You* know. So I says to Dot—come on let's go see what everybody's lookin' at.

So she says—Aw come on, we wantta get a good seat. So I says…haah? Course I don't let no broad crack the whip over me. *Come on* I say. So I pull her arm and we cross the street even though she don't wanna.

So there's a big crowd there, see? There's so many people I can't see what's up. So I taps a guy on the shoulder and I says—what's goin' on? *He* don't know. He gives me a shrug. Is it some guy drunk? I says to him. *He* don't know. He says he thinks it's some guy who ain't got on no clothes. Yeah! That's what the guy said. Woid fo' woid.

So Dot says—let's go, will ya? I give her the eye. *You* know. Cut it out I says. If there's a guy without no clothes, you'll be the first one'll wanna see it, I says. So she gets all snooty. You know, like all broads get. Sure.

So anyway, we stick around. I push more in the crowd so I can see. Everyone is kinda quiet. You know how crowds is when they're lookin' at somethin'. Like remember how quiet we all was when we was all watching old man Riley when the truck run over him? Yeah, that's right. Quiet like that.

So I keep shovin'. And Dot comes with me too. She knows what's good for 'er. She ain't givin' *me* up. Not with my dough she ain't. Bet your sweet…haah? Awright, awright, I'm tellin' ya, ain't I? Don't get 'em in a sling.

So we get up to the front practically and we see what's up.

It's a guy. Yeah. The guy had clothes on too. Yeah, ya slob, what didja think, I was gonna say he was bareass on Time Square? Haa haa, ya jerk!

So this guy has on like a bathin' suit see? Like made of fur. You know. Like Tarzan wears. But he don't look like no Tarzan. He looks like one of them apes Tarzan fights. Lots of muscles. Jeez he was more musclebound than them weight lifters down the "Y". Muscles all over 'im. *Covered* with 'em!

Covered with hair too. Like a ape. Ya know how cold it was last night? Well this guy wasn't even cold— that's how hairy he was.

But scared? Jeez, was he scared. Scared stiff. He had his back to a store window. You know the one, where they sell jewelry for ninety-nine cents. Yeah, near that t'eatre.

Inside the store this guy is starin' out at this other guy. This ape, this guy in Tarzan clothes. Yeah.

This guy has a club in his hand too. *Big* crappin' thing! Like a ballbat only lot fatter. Covered with bumps. Yeah. Like them cavemen used to carry. Yeah…haah? Wait a secon' will ya? I'll get to it. You ain't heard nothin' yet. This is a kick.

So we look at this jerk, see? Dot pulls back sort of. What's the matter I says to her, ya sorry he ain't got no clothes on? She don't say nothin'. Just looks white in the gills. Dames. You know.

So I turn to this old jerk next to me. I ask him—who is this guy? But he don't know.

Where'd he come from, I say to him. He shakes his head.

He looked cockeyed, this old jerk. He was staring at this other guy with the club. And his hands is closed like he was prayin' or somethin'. Yeah! Aah, ya meet 'em all over. 'Specially in Time Square. Ha! You said it Mack. Ain't it the truth?

So, anyway, where the hell am I? Haah? Oh, yeah.

So I ask this slob once more another question. I asks him how long he's standin' there. He turns and looks at me like he gonna jump me. Yeah. Jeez, Mack, no crap.

Then he says—just a little while. He turns away again and starts in starin' at the crazy guy with the club.

He has a book under his arm too. Whattaya mean who? The old jerk I mean. He keeps starin' at this guy with the club.

So Dot pulls my arm. Come on, she says, let's go. I pull away. Let go woman, I says. I want to see what goes. So I look up front again.

This hairy guy is showin' his teeth at everybody, see? Yeah. Like an animal. Some broads in the crowd is pullin' their dates back. Come *on*, come *on*, they're sayin'. Jeez. Broads. Ya can't argue with 'em. They're too dumb. *You* know.

Then someone says—*call* a cop. So I figure things're gonna get hot soon. Maybe there'll be a good fight, I says to Dot. So what does she do? Come on Mickey, she says, let's go see Frankie Laine. Laine Schmaine. Aah, fo' Chrissakes anyway. What can ya expect from a dame?

Haah? So I says to her—in a couple o' minutes. Can'tch wait a couple o' minutes? A cop'll come soon I says to her. Cops always stick their noses in when there's a crowd.

So I turn to a guy on the other side of me and I says to him—where did this guy come from?

Who the hell knows? he says. All I know is, I was walkin' by, all of a sudden, *bang*! There he is, standin' by the window.

So we look at the guy. Would ya look at the guy, says this guy. Look at those teeth. He looks like a caveman.

I'm getting' to that Mack. I'm *getting'* to it. Hold your water.

So I look at the guy with the club, see? His eyes is small. His chin sticks way out. He looks like…you remember the time we cut school that day. What day? Shut up a second and I'll tell you what day!

Man with a Club

You remember we went through Central Park and we went to that museum? You know, *way* up there. Around 80th street or somethin'. *I* don't know. Anyway, you remember those cases o' heads?

No, ya jerk, don't ya remember? It was upstairs someplace. Well, what the hell. Anyway, the heads showed what men looked like from the time they was apes.

So what? So this guy looked like what men looked like t'ousands o' years ago. Or millions. Who knows? Anyway, this guy looks like a caveman. Yeah.

Let's see. Where was I? Oh, yeah.

So I hear some guy say—this is hideous.

Yeah! Ha! This guy says—this is *hideous*. Ain't that a kick? Well who the hell d'you think? The *old jerk*! With his bible. I *did* so tell ya it was a bible. Awright, so I said he had a book. So I meant it was a bible.

So I look at this guy see? The old guy.

He looks like one of those jerks you see down in the Square. You know, giving the crap about—comes the revolution! *You* know. Reds. Yeah.

Anyway I figure I'll humor the old fart. So I says—where do ya think the guy come from?

Well, *holy Jeez*, if this guy doesn't give me the eye like I spit on his old lady or something.

Don't you know? he says to me. Don't you *see*?

Yeah. How do ya like that? Don't I *see*. See what fo' crap's sake? That's what *I* wanna know.

So I look the old jerk over. Some goddam Commie I figure. I would've give him the knee if there wasn't so many guys around.

Well, to make a long story short, all of a sudden the crowd *jumps back*! I get almost knocked down. Dot yells blue murder. Look out! someone else yells.

So I look up front.

The crazy guy is tryin' to jump some broad up front. He's *growlin'* at her. Yeah! Look, was I there or wasn't I? Well, shut up then. I was there. I saw the bastid with my own eyes. Take my woid.

The guy even unloads his club and takes a swat at the broad.

Yeah! That's right. Boy, what a kick. It was like a crappin' movie.

Get a cop, get a cop! the broads start yellin', jumpin', out o' their pants. They're all the same. Somethin' happens and they go runnin' for cops.

Yeah, and some old character is standin' in an ashcan and yellin'—Police! Police! Help, police! Yeah! Ya shoulda seen the slob. You woulda died.

So everybody is excited and the crowd's breakin' it up. But there's more crowds pushin' in, see? To see what's goin' on. So everybody's shovin' and pushin', pushin' and shovin'. Scene from a crappin' movie.

What? The guy with the club? Aah, he's back against the window again. Sure. His eyes is rollin' around like crazy. All the time he's showin' his teeth. It was a riot Mack, take it from me.

So somebody *gets* a cop. No, wait a second. That ain't all.

This cop pushes through the crowd, see? *Big* son of a bitch. You know the kind. All right, *break* it up, *break* it up, he says. Same old crap all the time. *Break* it up.

He comes up to the guy with the club.

And who do you think *you* are, he says, Superman? He gives the guy a shove. Come on ya bum, he says, you're under...

And all of a sudden, boppo! The guy swings his club and whacks the bull over the nut. *Jeez did he slug him!* The cop goes down like a sack of potatoes. Blood comes out his ears.

Everyone gives a yell. Dot grabs my hand and pulls me down towards Eight Avenue.

Man with a Club

But the guy isn't chasin' anybody. So I pulls away from Dot.

Come on Mickey, she says, let's go to the show. Is *she* scared. She's goin' in her…haah? Awright!

So I says I ain't missin' this for nothin'. What a broad.

You'd think a guy got a chance everyday to see a show like that.

She keeps whinin'. You *told* me you was takin' me to the Paramount, she says.

Look baby, I says, Look, you'll get to the Paramount, see? Just keep your pants on. Did I tell her right? What the hell. Ya can't let 'em walk on ya. Am I right or am I wrong?

Haah? Oh yeah.

Well I leave her down by the Automat down the street. I says I'll be right back. I just wanna get a good look at the knocked out cop.

So I go back. There isn't many people around. They was all scared I guess. Jeez how that guy cracked that cop! I could still hear it, Mack.

So the cop is out cold see? But there's *another* cop comin'. He has his gun out. Sure, whattaya think. You think they take a chance? Hell no. Pull out their rods. What do they care they might hit innocent bystanders. Aah, *you* know cops.

Stand back everybody! yells the cop. *Stand back!* Jeez. All the time! They say the same things.

So-o, I watch him move in on the guy with the club. He's still standin' by that store window. The caveman I'm talkin' about. Pay attention will ya!

So the cop says—*put down* that club if you value your life. Uh-huh. How do you like that?

Well this character just *growls*. He don't know what the hell the cop is talkin' about. He starts to *scream*. Like

43

a animal. Gets down in a crouch like Godoy used to, remember? Yeah.

Does he drop the club? Are you kiddin'? He has it in his mitt so tight you couldn't drag it out with ten horses. Yeah.

And he's kinda *bouncin'* on his feet too. Yeah. Like that ape in the movies, what the hell's its name?

Anyway, bouncin' and puffin'. Yeah. Jeez, it was funny. Ooop, ooop, ooop, the guy is sayin'. You shoulda been there.

So the cop holds up his gun, see?

I'm *warnin'* ya, he says. You put down that club and come along peaceably or else.

The guy growls.

Then, *get this*, the store's front door opens all of a sudden.

Officer, officer! yells the guy. Don't you shoot out my brand new window!

Laugh! I t'ought I'd die.

But the cop keeps comin'. Everybody's quiet and watchin'. All the cars are stopped. Horns was honkin'. This big crowd all around watchin' the cop movin' in on this crazy guy. Yeah, a regular scene.

Drop that club! says the cop. He takes another step.

The crazy guy jumps!

Bang! goes the rod. Tears a hole out the guy's right shoulder. He goes floppin' back. Falls on the sidewalk. Squirmin' around. Blood all over the place. Jeez what a mess.

Get this though!

Even with half his shoulder shot off, this guy *starts getting' up again*. Yeah! Jeez you never seen nothin' like it, I tell ya Mack. What stren'th!

Well the cop moves in fast and gives him a *whack* on the head with a butt. The guy goes down. But he gets up again! Honest I never seen such stren'th.

Man with a Club

He takes a swing at the cop with his left arm. The cop gives him another on the head. The guy goes down for good. He's *out*.

No wait, there's some more.

After the ambulance comes and they all get carried away, I go back to Dot. Sure, she's still there. Whattaya think? No dame is gonna run out on dough. Am I right or wrong?

So we start back up the street. I see the blood on the sidewalk. The slob from the store is tryin' to mop it up. Kills his business, see?

Then I notice, who's waking beside me but the old jerk with the bible.

Well whattaya say? I says to him, kiddin' him along. *You* know.

He looks at me. Doesn't say nothin', just looks at me like he was tryin' to figure where the hell *I* come from. A real character.

Where do you think the guy come from? I says to him.

So he stares at me. And, *get this Mack*, he says:
From the past.

Yeah! How do you like that? Wait though. That ain't the best part.

I give him the once over, see? Then, just before we reach the corner I says—From the past haah? and give 'him an elbow in the rib.

And he says—get this—*Maybe from the future!*

Yeah! What do ya do with guys like that? Ya put 'em away. That's right.

So me and Dot went to the Paramount. Wait, I'll tell ya.

Boy, hey, *that Frankie Laine!*

Professor Fritz and the Runaway House

Once there was an inventor named Professor Fritz. He had a helper named Willy and a cat named Manfred. They all lived together in a big house just outside the city.

One day Professor Fritz invented a blue powder to make things come to life.

"Give me something to bring to life," Professor Fritz said to Willy.

Willy got a red broom and put it on the inventing table. Professor Fritz sprinkled some blue powder on it.

"It's not doing anything," said Willy.

"Don't be so crazy impatient," said Professor Fritz. He sprinkled a little more blue powder on the broom.

Suddenly, the fur stood up on Manfred the cat.

Suddenly Willy's mouth opened wide. "Oh, wow," he said.

The red broom was getting up.

It stood on its straws and swayed back and forth. Then it jumped down to the floor and started hopping around.

"That's incredible!" said Willy.

"It's pretty good, all right," said Professor Fritz. "Give me something else to bring to life."

Willy took a hammer from his overalls pocket and put it on the inventing table. Professor Fritz sprinkled some blue powder on it and it jumped up.

Then Professor Fritz sprinkled some blue powder on a screwdriver and a flashlight and an empty soda bottle. They all started running around the top of the inventing table.

The hammer chased the screwdriver and hit it on the head.

The flashlight kept turning itself on and off and frightened the soda bottle so badly that it jumped off the table and broke into a hundred pieces. Manfred the cat yowled and jumped into Willy's back pocket.

Professor Fritz turned to the red broom which was still hopping around the floor.

"Hey, you!" he said. "Sweep up that broken glass, would you?"

"Maybe I will and maybe I won't," said the broom.

Professor Fritz got angry with the broom for talking back. He put down the jar of blue powder and started chasing the broom around the inventing room.

"Boy, when I catch you, you are going to get it!" said Professor Fritz.

"You have to catch me first!" said the broom.

Professor Fritz didn't notice that, when he had put down the jar of blue powder, he'd put it down right over his Bunsen burner.

Willy didn't notice it either because he was trying to do two things at once. He was trying to get Manfred the cat out of his back pocket and he was trying to keep the hammer from hitting the screwdriver.

All of a sudden, the jar of blue powder exploded with a terrific BOOM!

Everything that could shake shook. Everything that could break broke. And everything that could fly flew away in all directions.

When the blue smoke cleared away, Professor Fritz found himself hanging from the chandelier by his yellow suspenders. Manfred the cat was sitting on his shoulder.

Willy was leaning upside down against the wall with his head inside a wastepaper basket.

"Oh, wow, it's dark in here!" he said.

Professor Fritz dropped down from the chandelier and pulled the wastepaper basket off Willy's head.

"What happened?" asked Willy.

"I think my blue powder went boom," said Professor Fritz.

"Well, then, I guess that's the end of that," said Willy with a sigh of relief.

"The end, my crazy eye," said Professor Fritz. "Look."

Over on the inventing table, the microscope was hopping up and down. The Bunsen burner was turning somersaults. The rubber tubes were crawling all over like snakes. The scraps of broken glass were jumping around like popcorn. Even the inventing table was shaking.

"Now you did it," Willy said.

"Don't get so crazy bothered," said Professor Fritz, "I'll see to it."

He started toward the inventing table, then jumped back in surprise as the drawers popped out of it and all his pencils leaped to the floor. All his papers flew out like flocks of white birds.

"Hey you, stop!" yelled Professor Fritz.

He grabbed his butterfly net and he and Manfred started to chase the flapping papers. They could only catch two of them. The rest flew out the window and disappeared into the sky. Professor Fritz stamped his foot.

"All my inventing notes," he said.

Just then Willy cried out: "Professor Fritz!"

Professor Fritz turned around and saw Willy standing across the room. Willy had the door ajar and was peeking into the living room.

"Oh, wow," he said.

Professor Fritz hurried over to him. "What's the matter?" he demanded.

Willy threw open the door. "Look!" he said.

Everything in the living room had come to life. The sofa was waddling around. The armchairs and the tables were marching up and down. The television set was running in circles. The piano was stamping its feet like an impatient horse and all the window curtains were flapping.

"Now you did it!" Willy cried.

"Don't upset yourself," said Professor Fritz. "They will all calm down in a minute."

Instead of that, the furniture began to leave the room. The only one that couldn't get out was the sofa. No matter how hard it tried it just couldn't squeeze through the doorway.

All of a sudden, the books in the bookcase started jumping from the shelves and flopping across the rug. Little Women bumped into Tom Sawyer. Black Beauty trampled The Wizard of Oz. Hans Brinker skated over Pinocchio. The rug was covered with books pushing and shoving at each other. "Look out!" they cried and "Let me by!" and "One side, Buster!"

Now the records started falling off their shelves. They slipped from their holders and rolled across the room like black wheels. Manfred started after them, then changed his mind and jumped inside Willy's pocket again.

Next, the pictures fell down from the walls and hobbled out of the room, giggling to themselves. The telephone jumped off its table and started crawling away. It pulled at its wire so hard that the receiver fell off.

"Operator," said the voice.

"Don't bother me," growled the telephone.

At that moment, there was a loud thumping in the bedroom. Professor Fritz and Willy looked at each other.

"Not in there too!" said Willy in dismay.

"So we'll take a look," said Professor Fritz.

They ran across the living room and Professor Fritz threw open the bedroom door.

"Oh, wow," said Willy.

Both the beds were rocking back and forth. The bedside tables were tapping their feet. The bureau was butting its side against the wall and the lamps were spinning like tops.

"Boy, I really invented something this time," said Professor Fritz.

"You sure did," groaned Willy.

They both jumped back as the closet door flew open and all their suits and coats came rushing out. Trousers started cavorting around the room. Shirts and undershirts jumped from the bureau drawers and fluttered toward the window. All the clothes began to move at once, even shoes and socks.

"My long red underwear!" cried Willy, running after them. The long red underwear danced to the window, leaped out and disappeared.

"My slippers!" cried Professor Fritz. He and Manfred hurried after them but they darted under one of the beds and hid themselves.

Professor Fritz grabbed a fishing pole that was passing by and felt beneath the bed for his slippers. The slippers kicked the pole away.

"You better cut that out!" said Professor Fritz.

Just then, the sink came running out of the bathroom spouting water from its faucets. On its back, toothpaste was squeezing from its tube like a long, white, squishy worm.

"We'd better check the rest of the house!" cried Willy.

They ran into the kitchen.

"Oh, wow," groaned Willy.

The doors on the stove were flopping open, banging shut, flopping open, banging shut. The cupboard doors were opening and closing so fast that they made a wind.

Suddenly, the refrigerator door flew open and food started jumping out. Oranges and apples rolled across the floor. Boxes of cheese skidded and slipped. Bottles of milk crashed down, splashing milk on everything.

Professor Fritz began to chase a dish of cold chicken.

"Come back here!" he ordered, "You're my lunch!"

"How can you worry about lunch at a time like this?" cried Willy.

"I'm doing the best I can!" said Professor Fritz, grabbing the dish of chicken. "If things are going to run away like this, the least we can do is try to catch them!"

Putting down the dish of chicken, he grabbed some clothesline from a shelf and lassoed the table which was trying to sneak out the door. The table whinnied like a horse and reared up on its hind legs.

"Down, you crazy table!" cried Professor Fritz.

"Look out!" yelled Willy.

Professor Fritz whirled around just in time to see the stove come charging at him as fast as a locomotive. He jumped to one side and the stove went rushing past. The clothesline was torn from Professor Fritz's hands and, together, the stove and table galloped from the house.

"We're free!" they cried, "We're free!"

Professor Fritz and the Runaway House

"Boy, that was a close call," said Professor Fritz, nibbling on a piece of chicken.

Willy didn't answer him because he was watching the knives and forks and spoons. They were hopping from their drawer and dashing out of the kitchen. The pots and pans ran after them making a lot of racket. The toaster followed, ticking like a clock.

"Oh, wow," groaned Willy. "What's going to happen next?"

All of a sudden, the window shades began unrolling. The windows started to open and close. The doors flew open and slammed shut by themselves. The walls began to tremble. The ceilings began to shake. The floors began to rock and roll.

"I'll tell you what's going to happen next," said Professor Fritz, "The house, itself, is coming to life."

"Oh, no!" cried Willy.

"Oh, yes," said Professor Fitz. "And I think we'd better skedaddle fast."

He started for the door and Willy hurried after him with Manfred peeking out of his pocket. They ran outside and down the path to the sidewalk.

Just as they turned, they saw the entire house jump off its foundation and stagger into the street.

"Hey, you crazy house, come back here!" yelled Professor Fritz.

"Nuts to you!" answered the house.

Professor Fritz turned red.

"No house is going to talk to me like that!" he said. "Quick! Into the car!"

"What are we going to do?" asked Willy.

"We're going to chase it, that's what!" said Professor Fritz.

They jumped into the car and Professor Fritz started speeding after the house. As he drove, he leaned out the other window, warning the people ahead.

"Look out!" he cried. "Look out! Runaway house!"

Meanwhile, the furniture was racing into the city.

A man was standing on a corner waiting for the bus.

"Boy, am I tired," said the man to himself. "Would I like to sit down."

Just then one of Professor Fritz's armchairs came running down the street. It banged against the man so hard that, suddenly, he was sitting in it while it ran.

"Whoa!" yelled the man, "I'm not going this way!"

"You are now!" answered the chair.

A lady ran up to a policeman.

"Officer, officer!" she cried, "I just saw a kitchen stove crossing the street!"

"Sure you did, lady," said the policeman, patting her on the shoulder.

Two boys were sitting in school. Their teacher, Mr. Nutt, was telling them all about long division.

"I wish I was watching television," said one boy.

"You and me both," said the other boy.

Just then, Professor Fritz's television set burst through the classroom door, ran down the middle aisle and knocked the teacher right over his desk. Then it plugged itself in and started showing a western.

"Yay!" cried the children.

A truck driver ran up to the policeman.

"This may sound crazy," said the truck driver, "but I just had a head-on collision with a piano!"

The policeman stared at him.

"Is everybody around here going crazy?" he said to himself.

A man was mowing the grass in his backyard.

"Boy, am I thirsty," said the man. "I sure could use a glass of lemonade."

"Be my guest," said a voice behind him.

The man jumped around. There, standing in front of him, was Professor Fritz's refrigerator.

Professor Fritz and the Runaway House

"Where on earth did this refrigerator come from?" wondered the man.

"From just outside the city," said the refrigerator. And, quick as a wink, it threw open its door, splashed a pitcher of lemonade on the man and ran into the alley, laughing.

Two sign painters were sitting on their scaffold eating lunch.

"That's funny," said one of them to his friend. "I could have sworn I just saw a pair of long red underwear dancing across the roof of that building over there."

"You'd better get your eyes examined," said his friend.

A little girl ran up to the policeman.

"My dog just chased a pair of black shoes up a tree!" she cried.

"And both the shoes were sticking out their tongues!"

"Everybody around here is going crazy," said the policeman to himself.

Just then Professor Fritz's car skidded up to the curb.

"Has my house run past here by any chance?" Professor Fritz asked the policeman.

The policeman was just about to take Professor Fritz to the police station when there was a loud noise at the corner. The policeman looked in that direction and his mouth fell open.

Professor Fritz's house had just stopped for a red light.

"There it is, the crazy thing!" cried Professor Fritz.

The light turned green and the house rushed off again.

"Stop that house!" cried Professor Fritz, driving after it.

The policeman jumped on a motorcycle and roared after them. He shot past Professor Fritz's car and caught up with the speeding house.

"All right you, pull over to the curb!" ordered the policeman.

"Nuts to you too!" said the house and it threw a bowl of goldfish at the policeman. The bowl landed on the policeman's head and the goldfish started swimming around his nose and biting it.

This made the house laugh so hard that it didn't watch where it was going. Suddenly, it crashed against a big tree—KABOOM!! The roof went one way. The walls went another way. Everything fell off, fell apart, fell in and fell down. It made a lot of noise.

Professor Fritz and Willy and Manfred got out of their car and walked over to the wreckage.

"Boy, what a crazy mess," said Professor Fritz. "Not to mention all the furniture running around loose."

"I hope you learned your lesson," said Willy.

"Oh, sure I did," said Professor Fritz, "Next time I make things come to life, I'll make sure they don't get so fresh."

Willy groaned and sank down on what was left of the sofa.

"Oh, wow, what next?" he said.

"I don't even want to think about it," said the sofa.

Purge Among Peanuts

The zoo was almost empty as Mr. Jones walked slowly down the stairs with a scowl on his face. A seal bark caught his ear like the cough of an ancient smoker. He could smell the flood of freshly cut grass and the toasty scent of warm leaves.

He made a wry face.

He passed a daddy carrying a junior on his shoulders. History repeats, mused Mr. Jones without favor. Some junior was probably carried on Roman shoulders to the arena to see Christians get digested.

He passed a row of wastebaskets and looked at the empty Crackerjack boxes as though they were hollow souls.

He stopped in front of the seal pool. His glance touched the sign. With my salary, I should feed them, he thought. And as for annoying them, I have better things to do.

The sun was ingot bright. Mr. Jones stared dully at the cool green water. He thought there were worse things than being a seal.

Suddenly a black whiskery monster poked its head out of the water and honked its horn at Mr. Jones.

Aaah, *shut* up, thought Mr. Jones. Stop shoving. Everyday it's the same. Shove. Shove. I bet you love it you bum. Watch the doors! You and your goddam— watch the doors!

Then Mr. Jones smiled benignly at the seal.

Won't perform unless there are more people will you? You performer you. A black zoo fly sat down to rest on his elbow. He brushed it away impatiently and walked directly to the pheasant cage.

There were little boys looking at the birds. A poppa was feeding the birds. The sign said, do not feed. Mr. Jones sighed. Watch 'em gobble gobble, said the poppa to his blonde-haired angel child nodding mutely.

The pheasants looked around in bobhead curiosity.

Your pigeon cousins walk in freedom. You sit in the cage in glorious Technicolor. Walk on wet concrete. Nibble at popular peanuts. Watch the beady eyes and strut.

Yeah! Strut you little minx. I know you. Can't take a joke. Always, "Oh Behave Yourself Jonesy" or "What Would Your Wife Say If I Told Her?" or "I'll Tell The Boss On You." Well, the hell with you, you little minx, I know you.

Mr. Jones walked to the fox cage. He looked at the scrawny red excuse for the sign.

Well, they sure beat you. No more chases. No more holes to run in. Slide along the earth into the cool belly of the mountain, panting and sparkle-eyed; happy.

Mr. Jones pouted as he walked away from the red fox. The trees are green. I can see them through the bars.

He passed a truck of green acrid-in-the-nose hay. Why can't we eat hay? Relative anyway. A filled gap is a filled gap.

Purge Among Peanuts

Two pigeons scurried out from under his feet and continued their walk with gentle histrionics.

"Come *on*, come *on*," said Mr. Jones under his breath, snap it up. Watch the doors.

He stopped and looked between the thick bars at two great moldy buffalo. He saw two baby buffalo standing behind their parents. Born in a public park. Sign of the times.

"Buffalos!" came a little girl shriek.

Mr. Jones turned away in distaste. My daughter does not open her mouth like that when she is looking at something.

Mr. Jones said to himself: I wonder if animals talk. People say no but how do they know? He shrugged his shoulders and looked down at the dead stagnant water where the black bear was drinking.

You old bear. Really lap it up, don't you? You're quite a business-man, Mr. Gibbons. Oh, you *love* that don't you, you oily old bear. Then you get mad because someone disagrees. Just because I like to empty the wastebasket at noon and you like to do it at five. Don't know your business Jones! Don't know your business. Just because I like to empty the wastebasket at noon.

Old *bear*. I ought to quit. I ought to poke you one in those bloodshot eyes and say, So I don't know my business haah! Well let me tell *you* one thing. I know more about my business than you know about yours! And don't forget it. Huh!

Mr. Jones stamped his foot and almost waved a stern finger at the bear.

A mothervoice whined behind him:

"Alvah, have you urinated?"

Mr. Jones whirled with blazing eyes.

"Good god madam," he said acidly, "Have you no sense of proportion!"

Then, without an answer, he turned away and stalked off.

~~~~~~~~~~~~~~

Mr. Jones bent over a concrete fountain, sent a burst of brackish water into his throat. A little boy standing at an adjoining fountain was putting his finger over one of the holes and squirting a stream of water in the air. A mother yelled. Mr. Jones passed on, superior.

He hardly looked at the straggly reindeer carrying bent clothes trees on their skulls. Barely noticed the floppy kangaroos twitching with fat zoo flies. He left the sunlight and went into the dark stale animal house. Voices sounded hollow.

He passed a raccoon who stared at him from black-rimmed eyes and then padded out onto its sun porch.

He stopped and looked at the big tan wolf pacing restlessly. They exchanged kind glances.

I know what you're thinking. The people stand here and look at you. They think of Russia and Greta Garbo in a sleigh and you chasing it.

Well, someday they'll put hairy coats on men again and put them in cages. And you can stand outside.

And laugh with your eyes.

Feeling particularly compassionate, Mr. Jones idled over to the lion's cage. There was a righteous, eternal print on his features.

He gritted his teeth and winced as strident boyvoices rang in the silence and they surrounded him like a relentless army of red ants. He looked down at their wild hair with distaste.

"Hey Mr. Lion what are you doing?"

For Chrissake little man. Can't the king of beasts even take a leak in private? King of beasts. On exhibition for jokers.

Purge Among Peanuts

"Look at his ears!"

Yours ears, you little bastard, are not so hot either. Mr. Jones could not contain himself. He uttered a long shuddering, "Shhhhhhhh" and walked on, barely noticing the slopebacked puma stalking drunkenly around its cage.

As he stepped into the sunlight, he heard the seals barking loudly. They must have an audience. Slick glory seekers. Whiskered prima donnas. Watch the doors.

He walked to a rail and looked over.

The silent ones. The great black ones. Silent laughing mouths. Leather pendulum of a tail. Garden hose trunk. Floppy cabbage leaf ears.

He looked at the huge beasts swaying as they chewed chomp chomp on the hay. I wish she'd get a corset.

You look like hell darling. I'm sorry if it hurts your feelings. But what do you expect the way you eat? You're getting as big as an elephant.

Mr. Jones focused his eyes. He smiled.

"My god you *are* an elephant."

"Whud you say mistuh?" asked a little boy.

"What's it to you?" said Mr. Jones.

He left without an answer. He felt superbly witty. He stopped and waved by two pigeons. He passed two little boys with packs fastened to their shoulders.

The great outdoors haah fellas? Watch the cars. Don't step on anyone. Forest primeval.

Don't trip on beer bottles.

~~~~~~~~~~~~~

Mr. Jones breathed in the smell of warm leaves and found it not half bad. He conjectured briefly on whether sparrows have adams apples. He shrugged, felt very silly.

He stopped in front of a birdcage. He looked in.

His smile had no humor.

Tidy practical vultures. Nature's morticians. Doesn't cost a nickel for a dignified vulture funeral. No shrouds, sobbed eulogies, thick rugs, white faces, tuxedos or tears. No corteges of coffins. No nothing.

Mr. Jones stared at the ugly red head. He watched it rip the greenish guts from a fish.

Who put you here? he thought. Who said, I think people will get a bang out of watching a vulture rip dead flesh with his curved and bloody beak?

Oh, don't turn away dear bird. Have I offended? You can't help it. If you were put on earth to tidy up the dead, then who can shudder at your baneful carrion stare?

Hurry back to your fish. The zoo flies are making a black crawling pattern on the rotten death of it. Suck a lively beak. Go back you tired old redheaded hunchbacked and black-feathered monster. Eat your dead fish. Have no shame.

Have we?

Something burned in Mr. Jones' stomach. An anger that would not be revealed. An uncontrollable yearning to shout out meaningful words and tell everything.

But his mind would not shape the shapeless thoughts.

He walked thoughtfully into the monkey house and out again, hardly glancing at the mass orgies. He felt close to something very fine and he could not stop to look at the red behinds of hairy monkeys.

Mr. Jones stopped in front of a cage and looked in.

You look like a hyena, Crocuta Crocuta. I have several names like things in your world. You don't really laugh do you? Not here, there's nothing to laugh at. Sometimes I feel like crying.

Mr. Jones stopped momentarily to look at the skunk. He sniffed hard but smelled only warm leaves.

He smiled tenderly.

Purge Among Peanuts

He walked over to the seal pool. There were many people staring down and laughing at the black mischief.

Mr. Jones watched a while dispassionately. Then a particular dive caught his fancy and he smiled against his will.

A chuckle followed, bubbling through his lips and then his laughter was lost in the roar.

Man and beast, he thought, with sudden delightful clarity. The everturning diamond. The flash of facets. Light.

Then dark again.

The Prisoner

When he woke up he was lying on his right side. He felt a prickly wool blanket against his cheek. He saw a steel wall in front of his eyes.

He listened. Dead silence. His ears strained for a sound. There was nothing.

He became frightened. Lines sprang into his forehead.

He pushed up on one elbow and looked over his shoulder. The skin grew taut and pale on his lean face. He twisted around and dropped his legs heavily over the side of the bunk.

There was a stool with a tray on it; a tray of half-eaten food. He saw untouched roast chicken, fork scrapes in a mound of cold mashed potatoes, biscuit scraps in a puddle of greasy butter, an empty cup. The smell of cold food filled his nostrils.

His head snapped around. He gaped at the barred window, at the thick-barred door. He made frightened noises in his throat.

His shoes scraped on the hard floor. He was up, staggering. He fell against the wall and grabbed at the window bars above him. He couldn't see out of the window.

His body shook as he stumbled back and slid the tray of food onto the bunk. He dragged the stool to the wall. He clambered up on it awkwardly.

He looked out.

Gray skies, walls, barred windows, lumpy black spotlights, a courtyard far below. Drizzle hung like a shifting veil in the air.

His tongue moved. His eyes were round with shock.

"Uh?" he muttered thinly.

He slipped off the edge of the stool as it toppled over. His right knee crashed against the floor, his cheek scraped against the cold metal wall. He cried out in fear and pain.

He struggled up and fell against the bunk. He heard footsteps. He heard someone shout.

"Shut up!"

A fat man came up to the door. He was wearing a blue uniform. He had an angry look on his face. He looked through the bars at the prisoner.

"What's the matter with *you*?" he snarled.

The prisoner stared back. His mouth fell open. Saliva ran across his chin and dripped onto the floor.

"Well, well, well," said the man, with an ugly smile, "So it got to you at last, haah?"

He threw back his thick head and laughed. He laughed at the prisoner.

"Hey, Mac," he called. "Come 'ere. This you gotta see."

The Prisoner

More footsteps. The prisoner pushed up. He ran to the door.

"What am I doing here?" he asked, "Why am I here?"

The man laughed louder.

"Ha!" he cried, "Boy, did you crack."

"Shut up, will ya?" growled a voice down the corridor.

"Knock it off!" the guard yelled back.

Mac came up to the cell. He was an older man with graying hair. He looked in curiously. He saw the white-faced prisoner clutching the bars and staring out. He saw how white the prisoner's knuckles were.

"What is it?" he asked.

"Big boy has cracked," said Charlie, "Big boy has cracked wide open."

"What are you talking about?" asked the prisoner, his eyes flitting from one guard's face to the other. "Where am I? For God's sake, where am I?"

Charlie roared with laughter. Mac didn't laugh. He looked closely at the prisoner. His eyes narrowed.

"You know where you are, son," he said quietly, "Stop laughing, Charlie."

Charlie sputtered down.

"Man I can't help it. This bastard was so sure he wouldn't crack. Not *me* boy," he mimicked, "I'll sit in that goddamn chair with a smile on my face."

The prisoner's grayish lips parted.

"What?" he muttered. "What did you say?"

Charlie turned away. He stretched and grimaced, pushed a hand into his paunch.

"Woke me up," he said.

"What chair?" cried the prisoner, "What are you talking about?"

Charlie's stomach shook with laughter again.

"Oh, Christ, this is rich," he chuckled, "Richer than a Christmas cake."

Mac went up to the bars. He looked into the prisoner's face. He said, "Don't try to fool us, John Riley."

"Fool you?"

The prisoner's voice was incredulous. "What are you talking about? My name isn't John Riley."

The two men looked at each other. They heard Charlie plodding down the corridor talking to himself in amusement.

Mac turned aside.

"No," said the prisoner. "Don't go away."

Mac turned back.

"What are you trying to pull?" he asked, "You don't think you'll fool us, do you?"

The prisoner stared.

"Will you tell me where I am?" he asked, "For God's sake, tell me."

"You know where you are."

"I tell you…"

"Cut it, Riley!" commanded Mac, "You're wasting your time."

"I'm not Riley!" cried the prisoner. "For God's sake, I'm not Riley. My name is Phillip Johnson."

Mac shook his head slowly.

"And you was going to be so brave," he said.

The prisoner choked up. He looked as though he had a hundred things to say and they were all jumbled together in his throat.

"You want to see the priest again?" asked Mac.

"Again?" asked the prisoner.

Mac stepped closer and looked into the cell.

"Are you sick?" he asked.

The prisoner didn't answer. Mac looked at the tray.

The Prisoner

"You didn't eat the food we brought," he said. "You asked for it and we went to all that trouble and you didn't eat it. Why not?"

The prisoner looked at the tray, at Mac, then at the tray again. A sob broke in his chest.

"What am I doing here?" he begged, "I'm not a criminal, I'm..."

"Shut up for chrissake!" roared another prisoner.

"All right, all right, pipe down," Mac called down the corridor.

"Whassa matter?" someone sneered, "Did big boy wet his pants?"

Laughter. The prisoner looked at Mac.

"Look, will you listen?" he said, the words trembling in his throat.

Mac looked at him and shook his head slowly.

"Never figured on this did you, Riley?" he said.

"I'm not Riley!" cried the man. "My name is Johnson."

He pressed against the door, painful eagerness on his features. He licked his dry lips.

"Listen," he said. "I'm a scientist."

Mac smiled bitterly and shook his head again.

"Can't take it like a man, can you?" he said, "You're like all the rest for all your braggin' and struttin'."

The prisoner looked helpless.

"Listen," he muttered hoarsely.

"You listen to *me*," said Mac. "You have two hours, Riley."

"I told you I'm not..."

"Cut it! You have two hours. See if you can be a man in those two hours instead of a whining dog."

The prisoner's face was blank.

"You want to see the priest again?" Mac asked.

"No, I..." started the prisoner. He stopped. His throat tightened.

"Yes," he said. "I want to see the priest. Call him, will you?"

Mac nodded.

"I'll call him," he said. "In the meantime, keep your mouth shut."

The prisoner turned and shuffled back to the bunk. He sank down on it and stared at the floor.

Mac looked at him for a moment and then started down the hall.

"Whassa matter?" called one of the prisoners mockingly. "Did big boy wet his pants?"

The other prisoners laughed. Their laughter broke in waves over the slumped prisoner.

He got up and started to pace. He looked at the sky through the window. He stepped up to the cell door and looked up and down the hall.

Suddenly he smiled nervously.

"All right," he called out. "All right. It's very funny. I appreciate it. Now let me out of this rat trap."

Someone groaned. "Shut up, Riley!" someone else yelled.

His brow contracted.

"A joke's a joke," he said loudly. "But now I have to…"

He stopped, hearing fast footsteps on the corridor floor. Charlie's ungainly body hurried up and stopped before the cell.

"Are you gonna shut up?" he threatened, his pudgy lips outthrust. "Or do we give you a shot?"

The prisoner tried to smile.

"All right," he said. "All right, I'm properly subdued. Now come on," his voice rose. "Let me out."

"Any more crap outta you and it's the hypo," Charlie warned. He turned away.

"Always knew you was yellow," he said.

The Prisoner

"*Listen* to me, will you?" said the prisoner, "I'm Phillip Johnson. I'm a nuclear physicist."

Charlie's head snapped back and a wild laugh tore through his thick lips. His body shook.

"A nu-nucleeeee…" His voice died away in wheezing laughter.

"I tell you it's true," the prisoner shouted after him.

A mock groan rumbled in Charlie's throat. He hit himself on the forehead with his fleshy palm.

"What won't they think of next?" he said. His voice rang out down the corridor.

"You shut up too!" yelled another prisoner.

"Knock it off!" ordered Charlie, the smile gone, his face a chubby mask of belligerence.

"Is the priest coming?" he heard the prisoner call.

"Is the priest coming? Is the priest coming?" he mimicked. He pounded on his desk elatedly. He sank back in the revolving chair. It squeaked loudly as he leaned back. He groaned.

"Wake me up once more and you'll get the hypo!" he yelled down the corridor.

"Shut up!" yelled one of the other prisoners.

"Knock it off!" retorted Charlie.

The prisoner stood on the stool. He was looking out through the window. He watched the rain falling.

"Where am I?" he said.

~~~~~~~~~~~~

Mac and the priest stopped in front of the cell. Mac motioned to Charlie and Charlie pushed a button on the control board. The door slid open.

"Okay, Father," said Mac.

The priest went into the cell. He was short and stout. His face was red. It had a kind smile on it.

"Say, wantta hand me that tray, Father?" Mac asked.

The priest nodded silently. He picked up the tray and handed it to Mac.

"Thank you kindly, Father."

"Certainly."

The door shut behind the guard. He paused.

"Call out if he gets tough," he said.

"I'm sure he won't," said Father Shane, smiling at the prisoner who was standing by the wall, waiting for Mac to go.

Mac stood there a moment.

"Watch your step, Riley," he warned.

He moved out of sight. His footsteps echoed down the corridor.

Father Shane flinched as the prisoner hurried to his side.

"Now, my son…" he started.

"I'm not going to hit you, for God's sake," the prisoner said. "Listen to me, Father…"

"Suppose we sit down and relax," said the priest.

"What? Oh, all right. All right."

The prisoner sat down on the bunk. The priest went over and picked up the stool. Slowly he carried it to the side of the bunk. He placed it down softly in front of the prisoner.

"Listen to me," started the prisoner.

Father Shane lifted a restraining finger. He took out his broad white handkerchief and studiously polished the stool surface. The prisoner's hands twitched impatiently.

"For God's sake," he entreated.

"Yes," smiled the priest. "For His sake."

He settled his portly form on the stool. The periphery of his frame ran over the edges.

"Now," he said comfortingly.

The prisoner bit his lower lip.

"Listen to me," he said.

"Yes, John."

The Prisoner

"My name isn't John," snapped the prisoner.

The priest looked confused.

"Not..." he started.

"My name is Phillip Johnson."

The priest looked blank a moment. Then he smiled sadly.

"Why do you struggle, my son? Why can't you..."

"I tell you my name is Phillip Johnson. Will you listen?"

"But my son"

"Will you!"

Father Shane drew back in alarm.

"Will you shut that bastard up!" a voice said slowly and loudly in another cell.

Footsteps.

"Please don't go," begged the prisoner. "Please stay."

"If you promise to speak quietly and not disturb these other poor souls.

Mac appeared at the door.

"I promise, I promise," whispered the prisoner.

"What's the matter now?" Mac asked. He looked inquisitively at the priest.

"You wanna leave, Father?" he asked.

"No, no," said Father Shane. "We'll be all right. Riley has promised to..."

"I told you I'm not..."

The prisoner's voice broke off.

"What's that?" asked the priest.

"Nothing, nothing," muttered the prisoner, "Will you ask the guard to go away?"

The priest looked toward Mac. He nodded once, a smile shooting dimples into his red cheeks.

Mac left. The prisoner raised his head.

"Now, my son," said Father Shane. "Why is your soul troubled? Is it penitence you seek?"

The prisoner twisted his shoulders impatiently.

"Listen," he said. "Will you listen to me. Without speaking? Just listen and don't say anything."

"Of course, my son," the priest said. "That's why I'm here. However…"

"All right," said the prisoner. He shifted on the bunk. He leaned forward, his face drawn tight.

"Listen to me," he said, "My name isn't John Riley. My name is Phillip Johnson."

The priest looked pained.

""My son," he started.

"You said you'd listen," said the prisoner.

The priest lowered his eyelids. A martyred print stamped itself on his face.

"Speak then," he said.

"I'm a nuclear physicist. I…"

He stopped.

"What year is this?" he asked suddenly.

The priest looked at him. He smiled thinly.

"But surely you…"

"Please. *Please*. Tell me."

The priest looked mildly upset. He shrugged his sloping shoulders.

"1954," he said.

"What?" asked the prisoner. "Are you sure?" He stared at the priest. "Are you sure?" he repeated.

"My son, this is of no purpose."

"1954?"

The priest held back his irritation. He nodded.

"Yes, my son," he said.

"Then it's true," said the man.

"What, my son."

"Listen," said the prisoner. "Try to believe me. I'm a nuclear physicist. At least, I was in 1944."

"I don't understand," said the priest.

The Prisoner

"I worked in a secret fission plant deep in the Rocky Mountains."

"In the Rocky Mountains?"

"No one ever heard of it," said the prisoner. "It was never publicized. It was built in 1943 for experiments on nuclear fission."

"But Oak Ridge…"

"That was another one. It was strictly a limited venture. Mostly guesswork. Only a few people outside of the plant knew anything about it."

"But…"

"Listen. We were working with U-238."

The priest started to speak.

"That's an isotope of uranium. Constitutes the bulk of it; more than 99 percent. But there was no way to make it undergo fission. We were trying to make it do that. Do you understand…"

The priest's face reflected his confusion.

"Never mind," said the prisoner hurriedly. "It doesn't matter. What matters is that there was an explosion."

"An…"

"An explosion, an explosion."

"Oh. But…" faltered the priest.

"This was in 1944," said the prisoner. "That's…ten years ago. Now I wake up and I'm here in…where are we?"

"State Penitentiary," prompted the priest without thinking.

"Colorado?"

The priest shook his head.

"This is New York," he said.

The prisoner's left hand rose to his forehead. He ran nervous fingers through his hair.

"Two thousand miles," he muttered. "Ten years."

"My son…"

He looked at the priest.

"Don't you believe me?"

The priest smiled sadly. The prisoner gestured helplessly with his hands.

"What can I do to prove it? I know it sounds fantastic. Blown through time and space."

He knitted his brow.

"Maybe I didn't get blown through space and time. Maybe I was blown out of my mind. Maybe I became someone else. Maybe…"

"Listen to me, Riley."

The prisoner's face contorted angrily.

"I told you. I'm *not* Riley."

The priest lowered his head.

"Must you do this thing?" he asked, "Must you try so hard to escape justice?"

"Justice?" cried the prisoner. "For God's sake is this justice? I'm no criminal. I'm not even the man you say I am."

"Maybe we'd better pray together," said the priest.

The prisoner looked around desperately. He leaned forward and grasped the priest's shoulders.

"Don't…" started Father Shane.

"I'm not going to hurt you," said the prisoner impatiently. "Just tell me about this Riley. Who is he? All right, all right," he went on as the priest gave him an imploring look. "Who am I supposed to be? What's my background?"

"My son, why must you…"

"Will you *tell* me. For God's sake I'm to be execu— that's it isn't it? Isn't it?"

The priest nodded involuntarily.

"In less than two hours. Won't you do what I ask?"

The priest sighed.

"What's my education?" asked the prisoner.

The Prisoner

"I don't know," said Father Shane. "I don't know your education, your background, your family, or..."

"But it's not likely that John Riley would know nuclear physics is it?" inquired the prisoner anxiously. "Not likely is it?"

The priest shrugged slightly.

"I suppose not," he said.

"What did he...what did I do?"

The priest closed his eyes.

"Please," he said.

"What did I do?"

The priest clenched his teeth.

"You stole," he said. "You murdered."

The prisoner looked at him in astonishment. His throat contracted. Without realizing it, he clasped his hands together until the blood drained from them.

"Well," he mumbled, "If I...if *he* did these things, it's not likely he's an educated nuclear physicist is it?"

"Riley, I..."

"*Is* it!"

"No, no, I suppose not. What's the purpose of asking?"

"I *told* you. I can give you facts about nuclear physics. I can tell you things that you admit this Riley could never tell you."

The priest took a troubled breath.

"Look," the prisoner hurriedly explained. "Our trouble stemmed from the disparity between theory and fact. In theory the U-238 would capture a neutron and form a new isotope U-239 since the neutron would merely add to the mass of..."

"My son, this is useless."

"Useless!" cried the prisoner. "Why? *Why*? You tell me Riley couldn't know these things. Well, *I* know them. Can't you see that it means I'm not Riley. And if I became Riley, it was because of loss of memory. It was due to an explosion ten years ago that I had no control over."

Father Shane looked grim. He shook his head.

"That's right isn't it?" pleaded the prisoner.

"You may have read these things somewhere," said the priest. "You may have just remembered them in this time of stress. Believe me I'm not accusing you of…"

"I've told the truth!"

"You must struggle against this unmanly cowardice," said Father Shane. "Do you think I can't understand your fear of death? It is universal. It is…"

"Oh God, is it possible," moaned the prisoner. "Is it possible?"

The priest lowered his head.

"They can't execute me!" the prisoner said, clutching at the priest's dark coat. "I tell you I'm not Riley. I'm Phillip Johnson."

The priest said nothing. He made no resistance. His body jerked in the prisoner's grip. He prayed.

The prisoner let go and fell back against the wall with a thud.

"My God," he muttered. "Oh, my God, is there no one?"

The priest looked up at him.

"There is God," he said. "Let Him take you to His bosom. Pray for forgiveness."

The prisoner stared blankly at him.

"You don't understand," he said in a flat voice. "You just don't understand. I'm going to be executed."

His lips began to tremble.

"You don't believe me," he said. "You think I'm lying. Everyone thinks I'm lying."

Suddenly he looked up. He sat up.

"Mary!" he cried. "My wife. What about my wife?"

"You have no wife, Riley."

"No wife? Are you telling me I have no wife?"

"There's no point in continuing this, my son."

The Prisoner

The prisoner reached up despairing hands and drove them against his temples.

"My God, isn't there anyone to listen?"

"Yes," murmured the priest.

Footsteps again. There was loud grumbling from the other prisoners.

Charlie appeared.

"You better go, Father," he said. "It's no use. He don't want your help."

"I hate to leave the poor soul in this condition."

The prisoner jumped up and ran to the barred door. Charlie stepped back.

"Watch out," he threatened.

"Listen, will you call my wife?" begged the prisoner. "Will you? Our home is in Missouri, in St. Louis. The number is…

"Knock it off."

"You don't understand. My wife can explain everything. She can tell you who I really am."

Charlie grinned.

"By God, this is the best I ever seen," he said appreciatively.

"Will you call her?" said the prisoner.

"Go on. Get back in your cell."

The prisoner backed away. Charlie signaled and the door slid open. Father Shane went out, head lowered.

"I'll come back," he said.

"Won't you call my wife?" begged the prisoner.

The priest hesitated. Then, with a sigh, he stopped and took out a pad and pencil.

"What's the number?" he asked wearily.

The prisoner scuttled to the door.

"Don't waste your good time, Father," Charlie said.

The prisoner hurriedly told Father Shane the number.

"Are you sure you have it right?" he asked the priest, "Are you positive?" He repeated the number. The priest nodded.

"Tell her I...tell her I'm all right. Tell her I'm well and I'll be home as soon as...hurry! There isn't time. Get word to the governor or somebody."

The priest put his hand on the man's shaking shoulder.

"If there's no answer when I call," he said. "If no one is there, then will you stop this talk?"

"There will be. She'll be there. I know she'll be there."

"If she isn't."

"She will be."

The priest drew back his hand and walked down the corridor slowly, nodding at the other prisoners as he passed them. The prisoner watched him as long as he could.

Then he turned back. Charlie was grinning at him.

"You're the best one yet, all right," said Charlie.

The prisoner looked at him.

"Once there was a guy," recalled Charlie. "Said he ate a bomb. Said he'd blow the place sky high if we electrocuted him."

He chuckled at the recollection.

"We X-rayed him. He didn't swallow nothing. Except electricity later."

The prisoner turned away and went back to his bunk. He sank down on it.

"There was another one," said Charlie, raising his voice so the others could hear him. "Said he was Christ. Said he couldn't be killed. Said he'd get up in three days and come walkin', through the wall."

He rubbed his nose with a bunched fist.

"Ain't heard from him since," he snickered. "But I always keep an eye on the wall just in case."

The Prisoner

His chest throbbed with rumbling laughter.

"Now there was another one," he started. The prisoner looked at him with hate burning in his eyes. Charlie shrugged his shoulders and started back up the corridor. Then he turned and went back.

"We'll be giving you a haircut soon," he called in. "Any special way you'd like it?"

"Go away."

"Sideburns, maybe?" Charlie said, his fat face wrinkling in amusement. The prisoner turned his head and looked at the window.

"How about bangs?" asked Charlie. He laughed and turned back down the wall.

"Hey Mac, how about we give big boy some bangs?"

The prisoner bent over and pressed shaking palms over his eyes.

~~~~~~~~~~~~

The door was opening.

The prisoner shuddered and his head snapped up from the bunk. He stared dumbly at Mac and Charlie and the third man. The third man was carrying something in his hand.

"What do you want?" he asked thickly.

Charlie snickered.

"Man, this is rich," he said, "What do we want?"

His face shifted into a cruel leer. "We come to give you a haircut big boy."

"Where's the priest?"

"Out priesting," said Charlie.

"Shut up," Mac said irritably.

"I hope you're going to take this easy son," said the third man.

The skin tightened on the prisoner's skull. He backed against the wall.

"Wait a minute," he said fearfully. "You have the wrong man."

Charlie sputtered with laughter and reached down to grab him. The prisoner pulled back.

"No!" he cried, "Where's the priest?"

"Come *on*," snapped Charlie angrily.

The prisoner's eyes flew from Mac to the third man.

"You don't understand," he said hysterically. "The priest is calling my wife in St. Louis. She'll tell you all who I am. I'm not Riley. I'm Phillip Johnson."

"Come on, Riley," said Mac.

"Johnson, Johnson!"

"Johnson, Johnson come and get your hair cut Johnson, Johnson," chanted Charlie, grabbing the prisoner's arm.

"Let go of me!"

Charlie jerked him to his feet and twisted his arm around. His face was taut with vicious anger.

"Grab him," he snapped to Mac. Mac took hold of the prisoner's other arm.

"For God's sake, what do I have to do!" screamed the prisoner, writhing in their grip. "I'm not Johnson. I mean I'm not Riley."

"We heard you the first time," panted Charlie. "Come on. Shave him!"

They slammed the prisoner down on the bunk and twisted his arms behind him. He screamed until Charlie backhanded him across the mouth.

"Shut up!"

The prisoner sat trembling while his hair fluttered to the floor in dark heaps. Tufts of hair stuck to his eyebrows. A trickle of blood ran from the edge of his mouth. His eyes were stricken with horror.

The Prisoner

When the third man had finished on the prisoner's head, he bent down and slashed open his pants.

"Mmmm," he grunted. "Burned legs."

The prisoner jerked down his head and looked. His mouth formed soundless words. The he cried out.

"Flash burns! Can you see them? They're from an atomic explosion. *Now* will you believe me?"

Charlie grinned. They let go of the prisoner and he fell down on the bunk. He pushed up quickly and clutched at Mac's arm.

"You're intelligent," he said. "Look at my legs. Can't you see that they're flash burns?"

Mac picked the prisoner's fingers off his arm.

"Take it easy," he said.

The prisoner moved toward the third man.

"You saw them," he pleaded. "Don't you know a flash burn? Look. L-look. Take my word for it. It's a flash burn. No other kind of heat could make such scars. *Look at it*!"

"Sure, sure, sure," said Charlie moving into the corridor. "We'll take your word for it. We'll get your clothes and you can go right home to your wife in Saint Louis."

"I'm telling you they're flash burns!"

The three men were out of the cell. They slid the door shut. The prisoner reached through the bars and tried to stop them. Charlie punched his arm and shoved him back. The prisoner sprawled onto the bunk.

"For God's sake," he sobbed, his face twisted with childish frenzy. "What's the matter with you? Why don't you listen to me?"

He heard the men talking as they went down the corridor. He wept in the silence of his cell.

~~~~~~~~~~~~

After a while the priest came back. The prisoner looked up and saw him standing at the door. He stood up and ran to the door. He clutched at the priest's arm.

"You reached her? You reached her?"

The priest didn't say anything.

"You did, didn't you?"

"There was no one there by that name."

"What?"

"There was no wife of Phillip Johnson there. Now will you listen to me?"

"Then she moved. Of course! She left the city after I…after the explosion. You have to find her."

"There's no such person."

The prisoner stared at him in disbelief.

"But I told you…"

"I'm speaking truth. You're making it all up in a vain hope to cheat…"

"I'm not making it up! For God's sake listen to me. Can't you…wait, wait."

He held his right leg up.

"Look," he said eagerly. "These are flash burns. From an atomic explosion. Don't you see what that means?"

"Listen to me, my son."

"Don't you understand?"

"Will you listen to me?"

"Yes but…"

"Even if what you say is true…"

"It *is* true."

"Even if it is. You still committed the crimes you're here to pay for."

"*But it wasn't me!*"

"Can you prove it?" asked the priest.

"I…I…" faltered the prisoner. "These legs…"

"They're no proof."

"My wife…"

The Prisoner

"Where is she?"

"I don't know. But you can find her. She'll tell you. She can save me."

"I'm afraid there's nothing that can be done."

"But there has to be! Can't you look for my wife? Can't you get a stay of execution while you look for her? Look, I have friends, a lot of them. I'll give you all their addresses. I'll give you names of people who work for the government who…"

"What would I say, Riley?" interrupted the priest sharply.

"Johnson!"

"Whatever you wish to be called. What would I say to these people? I'm calling about a man who was in an explosion ten years ago? But he didn't die? He was blown into…"

He stopped.

"Can't you see?" he entreated. "You must face this. You're only making it more difficult for yourself."

"But…"

"Shall I come in and pray for you?"

The prisoner stared at him. Then the tautness sapped from his face and stance. He slumped visibly. He turned and staggered back to his bunk and fell down on it. He leaned against the wall and clutched his shirtfront with dead curled fingers.

"No hope," he said. "There's no hope. No one will believe me. No one."

~~~~~~~~~~~~

He was lying down on his bunk when the other two guards came. He was staring, glassy-eyed, at the wall. The priest was sitting on the stool and praying.

The prisoner didn't speak as they led him down the corridor, only once he raised his head and looked around as though all the world was a strange incomprehensible cruelty.

Then he lowered his head and shuffled mutely between the guards. The priest followed, hands folded, head lowered, his lips moving in silent prayer.

Later, when Mac and Charlie were playing cards the lights went out. They sat there waiting. They heard the other prisoners in death row stirring restlessly.

Then the lights went on.

"You deal," said Charlie.

The Last Blah in the Etc.

You are awake, pale thing, your muddy eyes perusing. There the ceiling, there the walls; security in plaster and paint, in parchment jiggled with coordinate lilies. Primo: *Lousigoddam wallpaper*. It is, has been and never more will be your opening reflection. Secundo: *Mildred isajerk*. This thought may continue.

Slumber-fogged, your gaze seeks out the clock. It has not clarioned the dawn. It is, indeed, not even cognizant of dawn's most rosy rise, its black arms pointing frozenly to midnight's XII—

—or *noon*! You start, eyes bugged and marbleized, mouth a precipitate sanctuary for some indigent gnat. *Wotnth'ell*! And—*snap*! Body parallel with mattress becomes body squared. You are—presto!—ninety degrees of male American athrob; a sitting inflammation. With a crunch of the cervix, a crackle of the clavicle, you look around the room, you look around the—

Silence. All and only silence. (Pallid thing)

"Mil!" you call. What, no sibilance of frizzling bacon, no scent of coffee? "Millie!" No savor of charred toast, no lilt of nagging on the air?

"Mildred!" *Wot'nth'blublazinghellis—*

Silence. Oh so silence.

Your brow is rill-eroded now. A curious dismay guerillas in your craw. Too silent this. Too—*deadly silent.* Yes?

"*MILDRED!*"

Ah, no reply, blanched thing. Your corn-cobbed toes compress the rug, your torso goes aloft, you find erection. "What's goin' on?" mumble you. You thump across the room, shanks athwart, terror tapping tunes along your spine. You reach the hall. "Mil!" you cry. No Mil. The hallway is your racetrack. You are Mercury and Ariel. You are Puck in pink pajamas. "Millie!" No Millie. You blunder like a village-razing mammoth through the chambers of your home. "Mildred!"

No—need I append?—Mildred.

In fact, nothing. Whether sign of exodus, Goinghometomother note or hint of counternatural removal. Pale thing, you are aghast. Panic rings the tocsin in your wooly brain. Where—eh?—is Mildred? Why—ask you—at noon, are you alone, self-wakened?

Noon? But see, the black arms still point alike.

The clock has stopped.

~~~~~~~~~~~~

Pulsing with alarm, you seek the phone, *le pachyderme en difficulté.* Digits clutch receiver, receiver cups ear. Hark; you listen. Your mouth is cavernized anew. Why?

Dead as the doornail. (proverbial) That's why.

"Hello," you state, regardless. You tap distress rhythms. "Hello! Hello! *Hey!*"

The Last Blah in the Etc.

No answer. (Achromatic you) You drop the dumb Bell and worry a channel to the windows. You yank the cord and up goes the shade, flapping in maniacal orbits around its roller and through this paneful frame you view the picture of your street.

Empty.

"Huh?" Your very word. "*Wot the—*"

Strange tides rise darkly. Terror is a blankness. It is cessation, emptiness; figures, fog-licked, hardly heard, vaguely seen. "Mil?" you mutter.

No Mil.

Dress! Probe! Nose out! Get to bottom! Resolution hammers manly nails; your framework bolsters. Up—you vow—and at them. There's an explanation for everything. (Of course) You are the captain of your shape, the master of your soles. Once more into the britches! Onward!

Etiolated thing.

Bones garbed *vitement*, feet ensconced in Thom McCann's, you plunge through bedroom, hall, living room, kitchen, out through doorway and—

The neighbors! *The crossthehallwhydon'ttheymindtheirowndambusiness* neighbors!

You arc the gap to their door, heartbeat a cardiac ragtime. Manifest really. (Séz you to you) Mil, Millie, Mildred, MILDRED has gone to pirate a dole of flour, a driblet of sugar. She laughs, blabbing and blabs, laughing with the neighbor's wife. She forgets old mortality. (*Oohwilugiverhell!*) And the phone lines suffer breach. *Q*: And the barren street? *A*: Nearby, a parade, a fire, an accident alluringly sanguineous and the neighborhood emptying to view it.

Only this and nothing more. (Rationalize chalky, poem-lifting you)

Forthwith: Skin-puffed knuckles harden, your hand is become a fist. Rap, rap, it goes. Inside, silence. Knock,

knock. Ditto. Bang, bang. Also. You bluff. "Hullo!" you call, "Anyone t'home?"

No reply. *Boom*! You teach the door a lesson. But nothing. Terror-veined fury claims you. You twist the knob, the door creaks open.

Consternation.

No Mildred, no neighbors. The kitchen devoid of all—save (shade of *Marie-Celeste*?) a skilletful of orange-eyed eyes, awash in sibilant butter; a flame-perched pot with a delicate volcano of coffee in its dome; a toaster ticking like a chrome-cased bomb; the table set.

"*Hey*." The cry drips feebly from your lips. "Where *is* everybody?" (Where, indeed?) You clump into the living room. Devoid. The bedrooms, all—bodiless. Your next remark, wan thing? I quote.

"What's goin' *on* here?" (*Un*—as you say—*quote*)

Now resolution finger-dangles from the sawed-edge cliff of fear. (*Quelle* tasty simile) standing at the window, heart an eighty-mile-an-hour piston, you gape down at the street again. Empty; so empty. Panic looms.

"No!" Underground resistance again. Chin up, gauntlet down. *Avant*! Socratic you will plumb this poser to its roots. This Too Shall Pass!

You betcha.

Whirling, you greyhound to the door and exit. Pegasus could not pass you on the stairs—or make more noise. Three flights cannon-balling and the vestibule is yours.

Confusion plus. Boxes bulging mail like any day. Delivered papers strewn as always. "Huh?" Your quasi-gibbous eyes peruse the headline. **FIND STARLET TORSO IN FIRKIN**. No answer there. You plunge into the street, exploring.

One vast length of nothing, sir. One spacious, side-walk-sided span of silence. (*Quelle* alliteration) In the middle of the street you stand, goggling. *Ovez*—nothing.

The Last Blah in the Etc.

Not one soul, one movement. You are alone—blank, marmoreal thing.

"*No!*" cries the hero—that's you. You slam the door in evidence's face. This cannot be! There Has To Be A Reasonable Explanation. Things Like This Just Don't Happen. (It says where?) Terror ricochets off reason's wall and comes back courage. You're off!

~~~~~~~~~~~~~

Ah, picture you, sallow, slapdash sleuth you are, running a forty-minute mile to Main Street, pulpy legs awaggle, breath like radiator steam; The Picture Of Durance In Gray. Alone the crypt-still thoroughfare you scud, hunting for a fellow soul.

Doorbell ringing is futility you've found; knocking, a bootless cause; peering in at windows, inutility at its primest. Worse than inutility—*guignol* with its actorless scenes of a.m. enterprise—food boiling, frying, toasting, poaching; tables set and stoves alive. And even, propped on sugar bowls, the morning papers.

But no one there to eat, serve, read.

Onward. (Every Effect Has Its Cause) (*Naturellement*)

Approaching Main Street you come upon a fresh obscurity. A halted car standing in its proper lane, hood still pulsing with engine tremors. Standing there as though its operator were waiting for the lights to change.

Empty though. (Ice mice batten on your heart) You waver beside its open window, staring in. A bag of groceries sags beside the driver's place; a morning paper next to that. **BUTT HOLDS STARLET** reads the headline. No aid there.

"I don't *get* it," you announce. (You will, discolored thing) Painpoints etch lines around your face. Your fingers tremble, your glands secrete.

91

Courage, mon passé.

You press on again, the, apace, return to take the car. Desperate dilemmas dictate desperate deeds. (*Quelle* something or other) Sliding in behind the wheel, you slap the gears into mesh (The hand brake isn't even out) and press the pedal mightily. The car leaps off with gas-fed growlings. The silence is undone.

A thought! Hunching forward, you finger prod a silvery radio button, then, leaning back, await.

A moment.

"Lo-ve," sings a woman, "*lo*-ve, *lo*-ve," in eerie oscillating weariness, "*Lo*-ve, *lo*-ve, *lo*-ve,"

Somewhere, a diamond needle, groove-imprisoned, pendulums the word, untouched because unheard. A city station too. Does that mean the city is tenantless? What about—

—the world? Yes, that too, (To you) dun, albescent, pale as witches thing.

"*Lo*-ve, *lo*-ve, *lo*-ve, *lo*-" You cut her off, poking in another button. Silence. Another button. Ditto. Another, the same. Another. "*Lo*-ve, *lo*-ve, *lo*-ve," You're back again. Eyes frozen grapes, you snap the radio off. Nothing but nerve impalings there.

Drive on. Drive on. Drive on and on.

Main Street's intersection. You signal for a turn, abash, draw in your arm. You turn—

—and, horror-tossed, slam on the brakes, stalling the motor. Breath hisses in and chills.

"*Gudgawd!*" (Literal translation)

"Til now there was a chamber in your brain that still housed disbelief. A chamber of contention with the facts. *Q*: So what was it? *A*: Everyone in town, by some strange rule of mob, was gone to view a movie star, the President, a fire, an accident, some incredible attraction. That was why the streets were empty, the houses extempore exited.

The Last Blah in the Etc.

But no. The length of Main Street is a humanless alley strewn with unmoving, engine-purring cars. You stare at this, candescence. You gape upon a people-reft world. You are struck dumb with cognizance.

"No," you mutter. (Yes) "Oh, no." (Oh, yes) "*No!*" (Ah, but yes)

Oozing, mindless, from the car, you stumble forth, stricken as a zombie. Legged on wooden struts you clump across the gutter, goggle-eyed. No, you insist, despite the obvious; No, it can't be true. Denial breeds traction though. And gestation nears completion. In cob-webbed wombs stirs lunacy.

"Hey!" you howl, "*Hey-ey!*"

Snarling, you leap the curb and elephant your way along the sidewalk.

First National Bank. You fling your jangled self into the pie-slice opening of its revolving door and, spinning a desperate arc, plunge inside. Yelling. "*Hey-ey!* HEY!"

Silence.

"HEY-EY!"

The aberration of your voice handballs off marble walls, ricochets from polished v.p. desk and wriggles, troublous, between the bars of empty teller cages.

Unnerving you. Whirling, hissing, shaking, you exit *à pas de géant* (Running like hell) too distraught to concentrate on stealing money.

The street again. You rush into a woman's shop, clods thumping on the rug. You race by rows of dress racks.

"Hey!" you call, "Anyone here!" No one. You exit.

An appliance store—row on row of stoves and sinks and washing machines—snowy headstones in a linoleum churchyard.

"Hello!" you shout, "Hel-*LO!*" No reply. (You'll crack soon)

93

Turning, you find the street again, ice cubes dancing in your stomach. A candy store. You dash against its newsstand and headlines leap at you. *STARLET WEDGED IN CRUSE; TORSO OF ACTRESS FOUND IN TUN; STARLET BODY IN DEMIJOHN*. And, on one, in tiny letters, near the bottom. *Strange Sighting.*

(Ain't it the way?—wan, wishy-washy thing?)

Where was I?

Oh. You tear your gaze away and stare into the candy store. Empty; silent. Cups and dishes strew the counter, unattended. And *hark*: behind the counter, a malted mixer buzzes like an outboard motor n the distance.

"No," you mutter. (Thirty-forty seconds at the outside) "No. Hello! *Dammit, Hel-LOOOOOO!*" fury adds its rabid spine to fear.

They can't do this to *you*!

~~~~~~~~~~~~

"*HEY-EY-EY-EY!*"

You stagger-swoop along the middle of Main Street, bypassing cars like raging tide around islands. "*HEY-EY!*" You cry havoc. "WHERE'N'TH'HELL *IS* EVERY-BODY!"

Breath gives out. A stitch (in time) pokes needle-points into your side. Pupils like worlds swimming in chaos, your eyes whip around, searching. There has to be *an answer*. Fury rises. *There has to be AN ANSWER!*

"There *has* to be!" you scream.

And, sired by malfunction, rage is born. (Right on schedule)

Hell-fire-eyed, you rush into a pottery shop.

"HEL-*LO!*" you challenge. No reply. Your lips compress.

"I said HEL-*LO!*" you ultimatum.

The Last Blah in the Etc.

No reply.

Pulsing with distemper, you grab a firkin mug and let fly. Strike one! A hand-wrought chafing dish explodes into china shrapnel. The floor is sprinkled with its splinters. Angry satisfaction fires your insides.

"*Well?*" you ask. Nothing.

Your hand shoots out and grabs a miniature patella. *Whiz-z-z-z!* — it goes. Ca-*rash*! Strike two! A hail of gold-fringed porringer fragments sprays the floor and wall."

"I SAID HELLO!" you shout. Not mad exactly; more infuriated than deranged. Arm extended, spar-like, you pound along the counter, sweeping trenchers, salvers, goblets, bowls and cylixs into one great Dresden bomb.

Which goes off with a glorious, ceramic detonation, pelting kaleidoscopic teeth just everywhere. *Strike three*! You are fulfilled.

"There!" you yell.

Whirling, profanations dancing on your tongue, you rush from the shop, laughing. (a laugh not wholly wholesome)

"HEY!" you cry, "HEY-EY!" You shuck out curses at the people-less stretch of Main Street. You jump into a running car and drive along the sidewalk for a block, making a right turn into the window of a furniture store.

"Look *out*!" You bound into the ruins and begin to topple chairs and sling sofa cushions at the chandeliers. "I said Hel-*LO*!" You kick in coffee table tops. You pick up porcelain lamps and pitch them at the walls. "HEL-L-*O*!"

And so on — hoary thing.

When next seen, hours later, you have run amuck, an abstract lamp shade for a hat, an ermine wrap around your camel's hair clad shoulders. You have burst into a supermarket with an axe and chopped pies and breads and cookies into floatsam. You have sent thirty cars running toward the neighboring town. You have thrown fistfuls

95

of hundred dollar bills off roofs. You have set fire to the fire department, then driven its ladder truck on Main Street, knocking over hydrants and lampposts, leaving it, finally, red and running, in the lobby of the *Gaiety Theatre*.

And now you sit, wearied with rage's labor, sprawled on a contour chair you've dragged into the street; watching your town go up in smoke. Thinking: Who cares, gawdammit, anyway, *who cares*?

Counterfeit Bills

Mr. William O. Cook decided that afternoon—it was raining and he was coming home from work on the bus—that it would be pleasant to be two people. He was 41 ½, 5'7", semi-bald, oval-bellied and bored. Schedule depressed him; routine gave him a pain where he lived. If, he visioned, one only had a spare self, one could assign all the duller activities of life—i.e. clerkship, husbandry, parenthood, etc.—to the double, retaining for ones own time, more pleasurable doings such as bleacher viewing, saloon haunting, corner ogling and covert visits to Madame Gogarty's pleasure pavilion across the tracks; except, of course, that, with a double, the visits wouldn't have to be covert.

Accordingly, Mr. Cook spent four years, six months, two days, $5,228.20, six thousand yards of wiring, three hundred and two radio tubes, a generator, reams of paper, dizzying mentation and the good will of his wife in assembling his duplication machine. This he completed one Sunday afternoon in autumn and, shortly after pot roast dinner with Maude and the five children, made a double of himself.

"Good evening," he said, extending his hand to the blinking copy.

His double shook hands with him and, shortly after, at Mr. Cook's request, went upstairs to watch television until bedtime while Mr. Cook climbed out the window over the coal bin, went to the nearest bar, had five fast, celebratory jolts, then took a cab to Madame Gogarty's where he enjoyed the blandishments of one Delilah Phryne, a red-headed former blonde of some twenty-seven years, thirty-eight inches and diverse talents.

The plan set in motion, life became a song. Until one evening when Mr. Cook's double cornered him in the cellar work room and demanded surcease with the words, "I can't stand it anymore, dammit!"

It ensued that he was as bored with that drab portion of Mr. Cook's life as Mr. Cook himself had been. No amount of reasonable threats prevailed. Faced with the prospect of being exposed by the sullen double, Mr. Cook—after discarding the alternate course of murdering himself by proxy—hit upon the idea of making a second duplicate in order to give the first one a chance to live.

This worked admirably until the second duplicate grew jaded and demanding. Mr. Cook tried to talk the two copies into alternating painful duty with pleasurable diversion; but, quite naturally, the first duplicate refused, enjoying the company of a Miss Gina Bonaroba of Madame Gogarty's too much to be willing to spend part of his time performing the mundane chores of everyday.

Cornered again, Mr. Cook reluctantly made a third duplicate; then a fourth, a fifth. The city, albeit large, soon became thick with William O. Cooks. He would come upon himself at corners, discover himself asking himself for lights, end up, quite literally, beside himself. Life grew complex. Yet Mr. Cook did not complain. Actually, he rather liked the company of his facsimiles and they often enjoyed quite pleasant bowling parties together. Then, of course, there was always Delilah and her estimable charms.

Which was what, ultimately, brought about the disaster.

One evening, on arriving at Madame Gogarty's, Mr. Cook found duplicate number seven in the willing arms of Delilah. Protest as the poor girl would that she had no idea it wasn't him, the infuriated Mr. Cook struck her, then as it were, himself. Meanwhile, down the hall, copy number three had come upon copy number five in the overwhelming embrace of both their favorite, a Miss Gertrude Leman. Another fist battle broke out during which duplicates number two and four arrived and joined in fiercely. The house soon rang with the cries of their composite battlings.

At this juncture, an incensed Madame Gogarty intervened. Following the breaking up of the brawl, she had Mr. Cook and his selves trailed to their house in the suburbs. That night, a trifle before midnight, there was an unexplained explosion in the cellar of that house. Arriving police and firemen found the ruins below strewn with bits mechanical and human. Mr. Cook, amidst hue and cry, was dragged to incarceration; Madame Gogarty was, grimly, satisfied. After all, she used to tell the girls over tea in later years, too many Cooks spoil the brothel.

1984 ½

Has it come yet?"

"No."

"Well—good Lord, where *is* it?"

"The man has other mail to deliver beside ours," she said.

"Well," he fumed, "I have to get to work."

"So get to work," she said, "Is it so important?"

"I like to look at it, *yes*," he said.

Rachel sighed. She went back into the livingroom and switched on the vacuum cleaner. Harold watched her for a moment, then glanced at his wrist watch irritably.

"Where in the name of—?" he muttered.

Rachel looked up as he shouted. She switched off the vacuum cleaner.

"What?" she asked.

"I said I'm going."

"Goodbye," she said.

It was on the dining room table when he got home that evening. Rachel had set it on his plate with a pink ribbon tied around it.

"Very funny," he said.

She didn't reply. Harold took his envelope into the livingroom and sat down, trying to look blasé. He heard Rachel go into the kitchen and, with a quick smile, he tore open the envelope and withdrew its contents. The bulletin fluttered open.

SELECTED United States Government PUBLICA-TIONS.

Harold's smile broadened. He wondered what sort of unusual pamphlets and booklets would be offered in this issue.

Could he help it if it intrigued him to run his eye down those lists? They had such fascinating titles. *The Pea Aphid And Its Control; Vitreous China Plumbing Fixtures; Hexagon-Head Cap Screws (Simplified Practice Recommendation); Tables Of The Gamma Function For Complex Arguments; What You Should Know About Rigid Vinyl Chloride.* Things like that. Bracing nuggets of information. Bracing, at least, to any open-minded person.

He'd learned a lot since subscribing to the bulleting. He knew, for instance, the geology of the Bighorn Canyon in Wyoming. He knew about intestinal coccidiosis in chickens, about the preservation of rocks, about auxiliary combustion, Lagrangian Coefficients, bunker silos and bituminized fibre sewer pipes. Rachel simply didn't understand. These were things people should be interested in.

Harold ran his eye down the new list penciling a mark beside *Weather Problems, 1924; Simple Cattle Breeding* and *The Preparation of Domestic Slime.*

Then he saw it.

1984 ½

Exciting Sex Practices In 1984½.

Open-mouthed, he read the explanatory paragraph.

Designed to bring together in a convenient form certain basic information regarding the strangely varied and exciting sex practices in 1984½. The primary purpose of this study is to provide male Americana with an adequate preparational survey of this vital subject and, in general, to present an objective appraisal of private participation possibilities.

"Ulp," said Harold.

He closed his mouth but it opened again. He felt his chest shudder with unnatural breath.

"*Lord,*" he said.

He twitched violently as Rachel came out of the kitchen and said, "Soup's on."

Folding the bulleting hastily and sliding it into his trouser pocket he stumbled upstairs to wash his hands.

"Anything interesting in the bulletin?" asked Rachel tartly as they began to eat.

"No. No," he mumbled, eyes fixed on his breaded cutlet. "That is," he amended, "There's a brochure on sorghum culture that looks good."

"How nice," said Rachel.

~~~~~~~~~~~~~~

It was not possible.

True, he'd seen listed in the bulletin such pamphlets as *Astronomical Phenomena, 1959* and *The American Nautical Almanac For 1958.* These were explicable. Men of science were limitedly prescient.

But 1984½? And—*that*?

Impossible. It was a misprint. What it was supposed to read was *Exciting S.E.C. Practices in 1944½.* Something like that. The compositor, myopic (or waggish—or both) had bungled the spelling.

That was all.

Harold stood brushing fluoric foam across his teeth and staring vacantly at his reflection. In the bedroom Rachel bubbled in sleep. It was after midnight.

No, I am *not* going to send for it!—declared Harold mentally. What, patronize base inclination? Obviously, the pamphlet did not exist; *could not* exist. Was he to send for it then and expose himself as a gross-thinking fool? Thousands of male bulletin subscribers would do that very thing, he doubted not. Perhaps even a few female ones.

Well, not *me*, decided Harold Rumsey.

A moment later he slid in beside Rachel and settled back on his pillow.

He came upon himself staring fixedly at the ceiling. 1984½?

~~~~~~~~~~~~

"Last night in your sleep," said Rachel, "you said, 'I *will* send for it'."

Harold dropped his English muffin.

"I who?" he said.

"You said 'I *will* send for it.'" said Rachel, "Send for what?"

"That, that, that, that—" machine-gunned Harold.

"What?" asked Rachel.

"That booklet on sorghum culture," Harold examined the depths of his Postum.

"Oh." Rachel finished her coffee and stood. She began to clear off the table.

"Lamb patties all right for tonight?" she asked.

"S-sure," said Harold.

~~~~~~~~~~~~

"*No*," he muttered.

"You spoke?" inquired Miss Finch.

Harold looked up from his desk, blinking. "Ma'am?"

"I believe you spoke," Miss Finch suggested.

"No," said Harold, "That is, I—I must have been daydreaming."

"I see." Miss Finch returned to her work. Dreams of whatever variety were unacceptable to her.

Harold removed his rimless glasses and polished at the lenses with a trembling Kleenex. Detestable, he thought. He must put the matter from his mind this instant.

"*And, in general,* he read over lunch, *to present an objective appraisal of private participation—*"

"*—possibilities,*" breathed Harold, unable to consider his peach-topped cottage cheese.

Well—by Heaven!—if such intangibles could be predicted almost thirty years ahead of their time, so, also, might others, reasoned Harold as he filled out the order form.

After all, wasn't it just possible that men *could* extrapolate into the distant future? And, as a cognizant human being, wasn't he obligated to investigate such momentous possibility? Of course! Beside, wasn't he sending for three other booklets too? It wasn't as if he was interested in only that one subject, was it? *No!*

He did hope it wouldn't arrive in one of those awful plain wrappers shrieking *PERSONAL*.

~~~~~~~~~~~~

It didn't.

There was nothing on the envelope but:

MATHESON UNCOLLECTED

Mr. Harold Rumsey
% Gabler & Karloff
Suite 209, Belcher Building
Los Angeles, Calif.

Well, was there any point in having it sent to the house? What if Rachel saw it? She was terribly naïve . No point in shocking her.

He didn't look at it all morning. He kept shoving the envelope from one part of his desk to another as if it were in the way. Finally, he shoved it into his topcoat pocket with a pettish "*There*." Now maybe he could get some work done. (Confounded envelope)

At noon, having accidentally incorporated the figure 1984½ seven times into his business calculations, Harold retired to a back table in *Bishop's Cafeteria* where, fronted by untouched spoon, cooling soup and warming salad, he withdrew the booklet from its envelope.

"Did you say yi?" inquired a passing busboy moments later.

Harold recoiled in his chair.

"*I beg your pardon*," he said.

"Nothing. I just thought you said yi," said the busboy.

Harold shut the booklet with vibrating fingers. He closed his eyes. Then he opened his eyes and the booklet and read again. Then he closed his eyes again and began to quake.

"Oh, yi," he whimpered.

~~~~~~~~~~~~~

As he hung up his topcoat that evening, the booklet fell out.

"What's that?" asked Rachel.

"A booklet entitled *You And The Alfalfa Weevil*," declared Harold. He picked it up and put it in his pocket.

"Me and the alfalfa weevil?" Rachel asked.

"No, *you*," said Harold, heading for the stairs, "The *general* you."

In the bathroom he held his wrist under cold water. "*Lord*," he muttered. That was a close one. Well, he had to protect her, didn't he? She was too fine to be exposed to such—such *saturnalia*.

"What's the matter, aren't you hungry?" asked Rachel over supper.

"I had a big lunch," said Harold.

From eight to eleven that night he locked himself in the cellar shop where, seated on his work bench, legs dangling, he studied the booklet.

Was it *possible*?—he speculated. Possible that men could actually predict the future in such detail?

Presuming that it was, why had they chosen such a topic? After all, anyone could send for this booklet. He, naturally, was interested only in the research aspects of it but—well, facts should be faced—there might be any number of those who would send for it out of less seemly motives. How in Heaven's name could the government offer such material?

How in Heaven's name had they *gotten* it?

He was staring glassily at one of the more pertinent passages when a knock sounded on the door and Rachel asked, "Coming to bed?"

"*What do you mean*?" charged Harold.

Rachel was still.

"I-I mean," he said. "That is, I'll—just finish up this mortise and tenon."

"Do," said Rachel.

After she'd gone Harold trudged upstairs, donned his pajamas and brushed his teeth.

"How's your planter coming?" Rachel asked as he sank down on the bed.

"My—?" He stared at her. "Oh. Fine, fine."

"That's nice," said Rachel, lowing her blinders. "Well, goodnight."

Harold looked over his shoulder at her. She was rather an attractive woman when you paid attention. Long, dark hair, well-formed features, ivory-like shoulders, full, rising-

In 1984½ one will be freely permitted to—

Harold shuddered. Hastily, he switched off the lamp and thudded back on his pillow. I must be losing my senses, he thought. Things like that just weren't—

Another 1984½ practice could be the mutual exchange of—

Harold flung himself over and buried his inflamed face in the pillow.

This from the government of the United States of America!

~~~~~~~~~~~~

I am going to stop *thinking* about it, vowed Harold, his breakfast postum turning to acid in his stomach.

"What's a double flip-flop?" Rachel asked, crunching bacon.

Harold went ashen. "A double—?"

"Flip-flop," finished Rachel. "You mumbled it in your sleep."

"I haven't the faintest *glug*," said Harold, addressing his last word to the cup.

Driving to work that morning he almost rammed two cars, one hydrant and an overweight receptionist from Glendora. Each time it was because he almost flung the booklet from his car, then, each time, relented.

1984 ½

When he arrived at the office there was an envelope from the United States Printing Office on his desk. That would be the rest of the pamphlets he'd sent for. He slid the envelope into his topcoat pocket, thinking that there was more to this situation than just personal outrage. The government was dealing in prophecies of a decidedly unwholesome nature. Excluding the immediate question of how they were doing it there remained the vital pertinence—Was this nefarious promulgation to go unopposed?

Not likely, resolved citizen Rumsey.

But where to begin? There was a definite flavor of conspiracy in this. If men in the government could actually predict the future should not the fact be emblazoned on the front pages of every newspaper in the country? Why should such a miracle be confined to a notation on a government publication bulletin?

And why such a subject?

But he wasn't going to think about that part of it. That wasn't—

A double flip-flop is an inspired combination of the Samurai demivolt and—

I say avaunt!—raged Harold within. There was some monstrous cabal afoot. No time for crudities.

~~~~~~~~~~~~

"Are you staring at me?" asked Rachel.

"What?" Harold twitched on the bed.

"You were staring at me." Rachel stood before him in the adhesive transparency of her nightgown.

"I—?" said Harold. "N-not at all. I was—thinking."

"Oh. I thought you were staring at me."

She turned and padded into the bathroom to wash her face. Harold exhaled gusty breath. Despicable, he thought. I've got to *watch* myself. He lay there staring at

Rachel's plump abundance. I wonder, the thought came, what it would be like to—

He jammed his eyes shut. "Con-*trol*," he muttered between gritted teeth.

A few minutes later Rachel flicked off the bathroom light and padded back to bed. Harold pretended to sleep. He felt the mattress yield beneath her settling weight, then heard the lamp switched off.

He opened his eyes. Next to him Rachel was twisting onto her side with a delicate sigh. He turned his head a bit and saw the dark outline of her beside him. He could reach out and—

Empathy twitched his hand. He forced his lids shut and countered. One-two-three-four—

"*Yi!*"

A gasping Rachel jerked her hand back from his chest.

"What are you *doing*?" demanded Harold.

"I was just going to—to kiss you goodnight," said Rachel, "Why?"

"*Nothing. Nothing.*"

"Are you cold?"

"*Of course not.*"

"You're shivering."

"*I am not shivering.*"

"Well, you needn't shout."

"*I am not shouting!*"

"You *are*."

Harold flung back the bedclothes and lurched to his feet.

"Where are you going?" asked Rachel.

"*To get a drink of water! Do you mind!*"

He stood twitching on the bathroom tiles and staring at his dazed reflection. This was *abominable*. That booklet was turning him into a ravening beast! What would poor Rachel *think*?

He'd read; that was it. There were those other booklets: *Sorghum Culture*. *The Poultry Grading Manual* and *The Romance of Grapefruit Pits*. He'd replace tainted thought with wholesome information, that's what he'd do.

His hand trembled in the pocket of his topcoat as he reached down for the envelope.

"You all right?" asked Rachel from the bed.

"*Yes. I'm all right.*"

He went downstairs to the livingroom and turned on his reading lamp. Now...

He sat numbly in his armchair staring at the letter.

Enclosed find three of the four booklets you ordered. We have on our list no booklet entitled Exciting Sex Practices In 1984½.

Harold blinked. But this was inexplicable. He'd already received the booklet. If the government hadn't sent it, then who—?

"Harold?"

His head jerked up. Rachel was standing on the bottom step, looking at him.

It came to him.

"*Impossible,*" he said.

Rachel lowered her green eyes. "I—guess you know," she murmured.

"*Impossible,*" said Harold.

"I know you must think I'm awful," Rachel said, "and terrible and—"

"*Impossible,*" said Harold.

"Well, *you're* impossible too!" Rachel flared, "You and those booklets of yours! We're supposed to be *married*, Harold. *Married!*"

He gaped at her. "But...*how?*" he asked.

"Oh." Rachel shrugged. "What's the difference? I had a counterfeit bulletin printed and burned the real one when it was delivered that day. I had the booklet printed."

"But—"

"I mailed it to your office," she anticipated his question, "because I knew you wouldn't have it sent it here."

"Oh," he said.

He stared at her.

"*Well*?" she defied.

"Those *things*," he said, hollowly, "Where—that is, *how*—?"

"Oh, I made them up," said Rachel pettishly.

"*All of them*?"

"I hate to disillusion you, Harold," she said, turning away, "but I haven't been living in a *closet* all my life."

"*Wait*."

She turned as he stood and took a hesitant step toward her. "It's just," he said, "—just that I always thought—"

"What too many men think," she finished for him. "That a wife isn't a woman."

Harold lowered his head. "You're right," he admitted, "I-I—"

When he looked up she was smiling at him, one hand outstretched for his.

"It's never," she reminded, "too late."

~~~~~~~~~~~~

"But how did you know I'd send for it," he asked a little later.

"I just assumed you would," she said, "If you hadn't I'd have *really* been worried."

"I didn't really say 'I *will* send for it' that night, did I?"

"Well," she confessed, "Maybe I did—prod you a little."

"Double flip-flop indeed," said Harold. Rachel giggled.

"Only one thing I don't understand," he said, "Where did you get *1984½*?"

When she told him he clapped himself on the forehead. "I *am* dense," he said.

Rachel laughed softly. "So you thought it meant the future?" she asked.

"Yes."

"How does it feel?" she asked. "to be the first time traveler?"

"I like it," murmured Harold, reaching for her again.

And there they were in *1984½* — Victory Boulevard, Los Angeles, California.

Pride

The flight from Honolulu arrived in Los Angeles at four-fifteen p.m. Bob stood up from his seat and took down their overnight bags from the bin, putting them on his seat. He smiled at Jeanne. "Nice flight," he said.

"We didn't have to go first class," she told him. "That was very extravagant of you."

"Are you kidding?" He chuckled. "On our honeymoon? Come on."

"I know but—"

She stood up beside him while everyone waited for the front exit door to open. Bob put an arm around her and kissed her on the cheek. "Have a good time?" he asked.

"I had a wonderful time," she said.

"Good." He put both arms around her and gave her a big kiss on the lips. The other passengers in First Class smiled and some of them clapped.

"Bob..." Jean was blushing. "Not here."

"Don't be silly," he said with mock sternness. "You're my wife now. I can kiss you anytime I want."

She smiled, embarrassed. "I know," she said.

"You're mine now, babe," he said.

She drew in a trembling breath. "I am," she whispered.

~~~~~~~~~~~~

The limousine driver was waiting for them as they exited the terminal. He was holding up a card that read THOMPSON. He smiled at them and took their overnight bags. "Have a good flight?" he asked.

"Had a perfect flight," Bob told him.

"Good," the limousine driver nodded and smiled.

They followed him through the terminal, heading for the luggage carousel.

"A limo too," Jeanne murmured. "They're so expensive."

"Enough, enough," Bob scolded her. "This was our honeymoon. It had to be first class all the way."

"It was, darling, it was," she said.

"Especially you know what," he said, suppressing a grin.

"Shh." Jean looked embarrassed again.

Bob laughed. "You're too much," he said. "You act as though we just met."

She leaned in close to him and whispered into his ear. "I almost gave in when we first met too," she confessed.

He put an arm around her and squeezed her tightly. "It's my devilish charm," he said.

She made a face. "It's something," she answered.

Bob laughed again, this time in satisfaction.

Pride

~~~~~~~~~~~~

They sat close together in the limousine, Bob's hand gripping her legs. Once he started to move it up to her groin she gasped in shocked surprise. "Bob," she murmured.

He looked at her with hooded eyes. "Why not?" he asked. "Why not right here? The driver is way up in front, he won't see." He reached down and started to unzip his pants.

"Bob, for God's sake," she whispered urgently. "Are you out of your mind?"

"Yes, I am," he said in a guttural voice. "Whenever I think of you naked and waiting."

She blushed again, looking at him with an expression more wanton than critical. "When we get home," she said.

"And all night," he said. "And all day tomorrow."

She reached down and put her hand on his crotch, squeezing at the hardness in his pants.

"Why not?" she said.

~~~~~~~~~~~~

When they reached the house, the limousine driver brought in their luggage and Bob gave him a twenty dollar tip.

"Why don't you unpack while I go get the kids at the sitter's house," he said.

"I'll get them," she said.

"Don't be silly," he told her. "Unpack."

He went outside, opened up the garage door and backed the Lexus out into the street, drove off.

~~~~~~~~~~~~

She stood in front of the fireplace mantel, looking at the photographs of Lise, Valerie and Jimmy. She wished the photograph didn't have Arnold in it. It was too bad that it was the best photograph of the kids she had. She'd thought of scissoring out Arnold's face after the separation and divorce but decided it would make the photograph look too strange. Anyway, he was still their father.

She drew in a deep sigh, gazing at the photograph. They were really beautiful children. It was unfortunate that they didn't care too much for Bob. He treated them pleasantly enough.

~~~~~~~~~~~~

At a little after five o'clock she heard the Lexus turn into the driveway. Moving to the window, she watched Bob coming up the walk to the front door.

She found herself forced to swallow before she could ask him how it went.

"Fine," he said casually. "No problems."

"They didn't mind?" she asked.

He looked at her accusingly. "What choice did they have?"

She nodded. "I know," she said.

"Stop fretting." He told her. "It was quick. I made sure of that."

"I'm glad," she said.

"Now..." He looked at her with a wicked grin. "Let's make us a family."

Now Die In It

They were in the kitchen when the phone rang. Don was whipping cream. He stopped turning the rotary beater and looked over at his wife.

"Get it, will you, honey?" he asked.

"All right."

Betty walked into the dining room, drying her hands. She stopped by the phone table. "Don't make it into butter now," she called back.

"Aye, aye, sir."

Smiling a little, she picked up the receiver and pushed back her reddish-blonde hair with the earpiece.

"Hello," she said.

"Don Tyler there?" a man's voice asked.

"No," she said, "You must have the wrong number."

The man laughed unpleasantly. "No, I guess not," he said.

"What number are you calling?" Betty asked.

119

The man coughed loudly and Betty pulled the receiver away from her ear with a grimace.

"Listen," the man said, hoarsely, "I wanna talk to Don Tyler."

"I'm sorry but—"

"You married to him?" interrupted the man.

"Look here, if you—"

I said I wanna talk t' Don." The man's voice rose in pitch and Betty heard a distinct break in it.

"Hold the line," she said, dumping the receiver unceremoniously on the table. She went back into the kitchen.

"Man says he wants Don," she said. "Don *Tyler* though."

"Oh?" Don grunted and started for the dining room. "Who is it?" he asked over his shoulder.

"*I* don't know," Betty said, starting to put cream on the chocolate pudding.

In the dining room she heard Don pick up the receiver and say hello. There was a moment's silence. She smoothed the cream over the surface of the glossy pudding.

"*What*!" Don's sudden cry made her start. She put down the cream bowl and went to the doorway. She looked at Don standing in the half-dark dining room, his face in a patch of light from the living-room lamp. His face was taut.

"Listen," he was saying. "I don't know what this is all about but—"

The man must have interrupted him. Betty saw Don's mouth twitch as he listened. His shoulders twisted.

"You're *crazy*!" he said suddenly, frowning. "I've never even *been* in Chicago!"

From where she stood, Betty could hear the angry sound of the man's voice over the phone. She moved into the dining room.

"Look," Don was explaining. "Look, get this straight, will you? My name is Martin, not Tyler. What are you—*listen*, I'm trying to tell you—"

The man cut him off again. Don drew in a ragged breath and gritted his teeth.

"*Look*," he said, sounding half-frightened now. "If this is a joke, I—"

Betty saw him wince as the phone clicked. He looked at the receiver incredulously, then put it down in its cradle and stared at it, his mouth slightly open.

"Don, what *is* it?"

He jumped at the sound of her voice. He turned and looked at her as she walked over and stood in front of him.

"Don?"

"I don't know," he muttered.

"Who *was* it?"

"I don't *know*, Betty," he said, his voice on edge.

"Well…what did he want?"

His face was blank as he answered her.

"He said he was going to kill me."

She picked up the towel with shaking fingers. "He said *what*?"

He looked at her without answering and their eyes held for a long, silent moment. Then he repeated it in a flat voice.

"But why, Don? *Why*?"

He shook his head slowly and swallowed.

"Do you think it's a joke?" she asked.

"He didn't sound like he was joking."

In the kitchen the clock buzzed once for eight-thirty. "We'd better call the police," Betty said.

He drew in a shaky breath.

"I guess so," he said, his voice worried and uncertain.

"Maybe it was one of the men from your office," she said, "You know they're always—"

She saw from the bleak expression on his face that she was wrong. She stood there restively, clutching the towel with numbed fingers. It seemed as if all the sounds in the house had stopped, as if everything were waiting.

"We'd better call the police," she said, her voice rising a little.

"Yes," he said.

"Well, *call* them," she said, nervously.

He seemed to snap out of it. He patted her on the shoulder and managed a thin smile.

"All right," he said. "Clear up the dishes. I'll call them."

At the kitchen door she turned back to face him. "You were never in Chicago, were you?" she asked.

"Of course not."

"I thought maybe you were there during the war."

"I was never there," he said.

She swallowed. "Well, be sure to tell them it's a mistake," she said. "Tell them the man asked for Tyler and your name is Martin. Don't forget to—"

"All right, Betty, all *right*."

"Sorry," she murmured and went back into the kitchen.

She heard his low voice in the dining room, then the receiver being put down. Footsteps; he came back into the kitchen.

"What did they say?" she asked.

"They said it was probably some crank."

"They're coming over though, aren't they?"

"Probably."

"Probably! Don, for God's sake—!" Her voice broke off in frightened exasperation.

"They'll come," he said then.

"That man said he was going to—"

"They'll *come*," he interrupted, almost angrily.

"I should hope so."

In the silence, he pulled down a towel from the rack and started drying glasses. She kept washing the dishes, rinsing them and standing them in the rack to dry.

"Do you want any pudding?" she asked.

He shook his head. She put the pudding bowl into the refrigerator, then turned, her hand still on the door handle and looked at him.

"Haven't you any idea who it might be?"

"I *said* I didn't," he answered.

Her mouth tightened. "Don't wake up Billy," she said, quietly.

He turned to face the cabinet and put glasses on the shelf.

"I'm sorry," he said. "I'm nervous. It isn't everyday that—" He broke off and started drying the dishes, wooden-like.

"It'll be all right, sweetheart," she said. "As long as you say the police are coming."

"Yeah," he said, without conviction.

She went back to her work and the only sound in the kitchen was that of dishes, glass and silverware being handled. Outside, a cold November wind blew across the house.

She gasped as Don put down a glass so hard it cracked. "What *is* it?" she asked.

"I just thought," he said, "that he might have been calling from the corner drug store."

She dried her hands automatically. "What are we going to do?" she asked. "What if the police don't come in time?"

She followed as he ran into the dining room. He started turning off the living room lamps and she turned and ran back, her nervous fingers pushing down the wall switch in the kitchen. The fluorescent tube went out and she stood there trembling in the dark kitchen until she heard him come back in.

"Call the police again," she said in a low, guarded voice as if the man were already lurking nearby.

"It wouldn't do any good," he answered, "They—"

"Try."

"Christ, the upstairs light!" he said.

He ran out of the kitchen and she heard him jumping up the carpeted steps. She moved into the dining room, legs trembling. Upstairs she heard Don close the door to Billy's room quietly. She hurried for the stairs.

She was about to start up when, suddenly, she heard Don's footsteps cease.

Someone was ringing the front doorbell.

~~~~~~~~~~~~~

He came down the stairs.

"Is it him? Do you think it's him?" she asked.

"I don't know." He stood beside her without moving.

"What if Billy wakes up?"

"What?"

"He'll cry if he wakes up. You know how afraid he is of the dark."

"I'll see who it is," Don said.

He moved silently across the living room rug and she followed a few feet, then stopped. He stood against the wall and looked out through the window curtains. Rays of light from the street lamp fell across the brick porch.

"Can you see?" she asked as quietly as she could. "Is it him?"

He took a heavy, shaking breath in the darkness. "It's him."

She stood in the middle of the living room and it seemed as if all the heat in the house had suddenly disappeared. She shuddered.

The doorbell kept ringing.

"Maybe it's the police," she said nervously.

"No. It's not."

They stood there silently a moment and the buzzing stopped.

"What are we going to *do*?" she asked.

He didn't answer.

"If we opened the door, wouldn't he—?" She heard the sound he made and didn't finish. "Why should he make such a mistake with *you*? Why?"

His breath sucked in. "Damn it," he muttered.

"What?"

He was already moving for the front door—and her mind was seared by the sudden thought—*it isn't locked*.

She watched Don stoop and take off his shoes. He moved quietly into the front hall. She closed her eyes and listened tensely. Didn't the man hear that slight clicking as Don turned the lock? Her throat moved convulsively. How did Don know it wasn't a detective? Would a man intent on murder ring the doorbell of the man he intended to—

Then she saw a dark figure standing at the front windows trying to look in, and froze where she stood.

Don came back from the hall. "I think he—" he began to say.

"*Shhh!*"

He stiffened and, as if he knew, turned his head quickly toward the living room window. It was so still that Betty heard his dry swallow distinctively.

Then the shadow moved away from the window and Betty realized that she'd been holding her breath. She let it escape, her chest shuddering as she exhaled.

"I'd better get my gun," Don said in a husky voice.
She started then. "Your—?"

"I hope it works. I haven't cleaned it in a long time."

Don pushed by her. She heard him bounding up the stairs. She stood paralyzed.

Upstairs, she heard Billy crying.

She backed out of the kitchen and felt her way to the stairs, her eyes always on the kitchen, in her ears the sound of the man trying to get in the house to kill Don.

At the top of the stairs, Don came around the wall edge and almost collided with her.

"What are you *doing*?" he snapped.

"I heard Billy crying."

She heard something snap in the darkness and realized that he'd set the hammer of his army automatic.

"Didn't you tell the police that he said he was going to *kill* you?"

"I told them."

"Well, where are they, then?"

Her words choked off. The man was breaking through a back window.

She stood mute, listening to the fragments of window spatter on the kitchen linoleum.

"*What are we going to do*?" Her whisper shook in the darkness.

He pulled away from her grip and moved down the stairs without a sound. She heard his shoeless feet pad cross the dining room rug. In the kitchen the man was clambering through the window. She gripped the banister until her hand hurt.

There was a rush of sight and sounds.

The kitchen light flickered on. Don leaped from the wall and pointed the gun at something in the kitchen. "Drop it!" he ordered. The house was filled with the roar of a gun and something crashed in the front room.

Then Betty sank down on the steps in a nerveless crouch as Don's pistol only clicked and she saw it drop from his hand. Between the banister posts she saw him standing in the light that flooded from the kitchen.

The man in the kitchen laughed.

"Got you," he said. "I got you now."

"No!" She didn't even realize that she'd cried out. All she knew was that Don was staring up at her, his white face helpless in the kitchen light. The man looked up at her.

"Turn on the light," the man told Don. His throat seemed clogged; all the words came out thick and indistinct.

The dining room light went on. Betty stared at a man with lank, black hair, white face, an unkempt tweed suit with an egg-spotted vest buttoned to the top. The dark revolver he held in a claw of hand.

"Come down here," he told her.

She went down the steps. The man backed into the kitchen, kicking aside Don's gun.

"Get in here, both of you," he ordered.

In the fluorescent light, the man's pocked face looked even whiter and grimier. His lips kept drawing back from his teeth as he sniffed. He kept clearing his throat.

"Well, I got you," he repeated.

"You don't understand," Betty was able to speak at last. "You've made a mistake. Our name is Martin, not Tyler."

The man paid no attention to her. He looked straight at Don.

"Thought you could change your name, I wouldn't find you, huh?" he said. His eyes glittered. He coughed once, his chest lurching, spots of red rising in his puffed-out cheeks.

"You've got the wrong man," Don said quietly. "My name is Martin."

"That's not what it was in the old days, is it?" the man said hoarsely.

Betty glanced at Don, saw his face go slack. Something cold gripped her insides.

"I don't know what you're talking about," Don said.

"Oh, don't you!" snarled the man. "It was okay so long as the riding was high, wasn't it, Donsy boy. Soon as things got hot you cut out quick enough, didn't you? Didn't you, you son-of-a-"

She didn't dare speak. Her eyes fled from the man's face to Don's and back again, her mind jumping in ten different directions at once. Why didn't Don *say* something?

"You know what they did t'us?" the man went on in a flat voice. "You know what they did? Sent us up for ten years. Ten years; *count* 'em." His smile was crooked. "But not you, Donsy boy. Not you."

"Don." Betty said. He didn't look at her.

"And you got married," said the man, the gun shaking in his hand. "You got *married*. Ain't that—"

A cough shook his body. For a second, his eyes filled with tears and he stepped back quickly and banged against the table. Then, in an instant, he stood, legs wide apart, holding the gun out before him, rubbing the tears from his pale cheeks.

"*Get back*," he warned. They hadn't moved. His eyes widened, then his face grew suddenly taut. "Well, I'm gonna kill you," he said. "I'm gonna kill you."

"Mister, you got—" Don began.

"Shut up!" screamed the man.

Then he was quiet, his dark eyes peering toward the dining room, the stairs. He was listening to Billy crying again.

"You got a kid," the man said slowly.

"*No*." Betty said it suddenly. She stared at the impossible face of the impossible man who had just said he was going to kill her husband, who was asking with unholy interest about her son.

"This is gonna be a *pleasure*," said the man. "I'm gonna pay you back good for what you done t'me."

She saw Don's face whiten, heard his voice, frail and unbelieving. "What do you mean?"

"Get in the dining room," the man said.

They backed into the next room, their eyes never leaving the man's pock-marked face. Betty's heart thudded. She shivered without control at the sound of Billy's crying.

"You're not—"

"Get up the stairs." A violent cough shook the man.

Betty shuddered as Don's hand gripped her left arm. She glanced over at him dazedly but he didn't return her look. He was holding her back from the stairs.

"You're not going to hurt my boy," he said, his voice husky.

The man prodded with his gun and Don backed up a step. Betty moved beside him. They went up another step and with each upward movement, Betty felt waves of horror grow stronger in her.

"Simpson, kill *me*," Don begged suddenly. "Leave my boy alone."

Don knew his name. Betty slumped against the wall weakly with the knowledge that everything the man had said was true. True.

"I *swear* to you!" Don said.

"Swear!" the man shouted at him, "Twelve years I been after you. Ten in stir and two years running you down!"

Suddenly his face was convulsed with coughing; he shot out his left hand for the banister.

In the same second, Don leaped.

Betty felt a scream tear from her throat as the roar of the gun deafened her. She heard Don cry out in pain and watched in rigid horror as the two men grappled on the stairway just below her. She saw blood running down Don's shirt and splashing on the green-carpeted steps.

Her eyes grew wide as she watched the man's hate-tortured face grow hard, the flesh seeming to tighten as if drawn at the edges by screws. The two men made no sound, only gasped in each other's faces. Their hands, wrestling for the gun, were hidden from her.

Another deafening roar.

The two men stood straight, staring at each other. Then the man's mouth opened and spittle ran across his unshaven chin. He toppled backwards down the steps and landed in a crumpled heap on the landing. His dead eyes stared up at them.

For a long while, Betty stood quite still.

Then she left the room and went back into the hall, closing the door quietly behind her. She went to the bathroom and got the medical kit.

Don was sitting on a step hallway downstairs, his head propped on two blood-drained fists, his elbows resting on his knees. He didn't turn as she came down the steps.

She sat down beside him and drew a bandage tight around his shoulder and arm.

"Does it hurt?" she asked dully.

He shook his head.

"I wonder if the neighbors heard," she said.

"They must have," he said. "You'd better call the police."

Her fingers grew still on the bandage. "You didn't call them before, did you?"

"No."

He began to speak slowly, without looking at her.

"When I was just a kid," he said. "Eighteen, nineteen—I worked the rackets in Chicago." He looked down at the dead man. "Simpson was one of the guys I worked with. He was always hot-headed, maybe a little crazy."

His head fell forward. "Well, when the police caught up with us I..." He let out a slow, tired breath. "I got scared and ran. I didn't think then either. I was just a kid and I was scared. So I ran."

She looked at him thinking how strange it was to have been married nine years to a man she didn't know about.

"The rest is simple," he said. "I changed my name, I tried to live a decent life, an honest one. I tried to forget." He shook his head defeatedly. "I don't know how he found me." He swallowed. "It doesn't matter, really. You'd better call the police. Before somebody else does."

She finished the bandage and stood. She went down the steps, avoiding the sight of the man lying there with his blood-soaked chest.

She dialed the operator. "Police," she said and waited, looking up at Don's pale face looking at her between the posts of the banister. He looked like a frightened boy who'd been chased and punished and knew that he deserved it.

"Thirteenth precinct," said the man's voice on the phone.

"I'd like to report a shooting," Betty said.

The man took the address. Betty's eyes were on Don, on the look of resignation on his face.

"The man broke into our house," she said.

"No," Don said, "Tell them the truth."

"That's right," she said, "We never saw him before. I guess he was a burglar. Most of our lights were out. We were watching television. I guess he thought we weren't home."

Don sagged and closed his eyes as she told the police to bring a doctor. Then, after she hung up she stood looking down at him.

"All right," he murmured.

The blood started oozing through his bandage then and Betty went and got a clean towel from the linen closet. She went back and sat beside her husband and held the towel against his shoulder until the flow stopped. Then she got up, went to Billy's bedroom and rocked him gently in her arms.

Downstairs, Don waited quietly for the men to come and take away the body.

Leo Rising

Grace?"

She stopped and looked across her shoulder. Miles was standing in the doorway of his study.

"Yes?" she asked.

"I have to speak to you," he told her.

No, she thought. She almost groaned aloud. Not *another* crisis.

"Please," he said. His tone was grim.

"The car's already waiting," she objected.

Miles shuddered. "This is absolutely vital."

Grace sighed and shut the front door. Give me strength, she thought as she crossed the entry hall. Miles stepped aside, admitting her to his study. "I have an awful lot of shopping to do," she said.

"This won't take long."

She cast her eyes upward.

Famous last words, she thought; he used them every time—and it always took long.

His astrological chart was on the desk.

"This is *it*," said Miles.

She held herself in check. "What's wrong?" she asked. *This* time? she kept herself from adding.

"An ultimate array of squares, semisquares, and adverse conjunctions," Miles answered in a quavering voice.

Don't sigh wearily, she told herself firmly. "What does it mean?" she asked, adopting a solicitous tone.

"Financial ruin."

She blinked. Did he say ruin? "Ruin?"

"Ruin."

Grace's mouth opened and closed without a sound. This was serious. With his fanatical devotion to astrology he might very well create that ruin just to prove his point. She stared at him in shock. All the aggravations of the past seemed trivial compared to this.

"See here," he said. He drew her to the desk and pointed at his chart with stabbing motions. "Square to Mars. Square to Saturn. Adverse conjunction. Semisquare to Mercury. Good God, it's a positive blueprint for bankruptcy!"

No, she thought. She could not repress a groan this time. And there was nothing she could do; that was the nightmare. In every other detail of their marriage Miles deferred to her completely. But where astrology was concerned—

"What are you going to do?" she murmured.

"It's already done," he answered. His voice made her shiver.

Incredible, she thought ten minutes later as she rode into the city. All these years of being convinced that astrology was nonsense. Now this. It certainly gave one a sense of cosmic awe.

"Where to?" the chauffeur asked.

Grace blinked and looked at him. "The bank," she said. She had to smile. *Your chart is free of such afflictions, don't you see*, Miles had told her dramatically; *therefore, to protect myself from this impending ruin I must transfer everything to you.*

"And then?" the chauffeur broke into her train of thought.

The sight of his shoulders and curly black hair made her tingle with anticipation.

"And then the airport," she replied, "Leo, darling."

Where There's a Will

Written with Richard Christian Matheson

It is not unusual for a son to follow in the writing foot-steps of his father, but it's uncommon for the two to col-laborate. Here is a rare and fortunate exception. Richard Matheson is a successful Hollywood screenwriter, author of many classic throat-gripping short stories and novels of terror—"Duel," "Prey," A Stir of Echoes, The Shrink-ing Man, I Am Legend—*as well as one of the key writers to work with the late Rod Serling on the famous* Twilight Zone *television series. His son, Richard Christian Math-eson, still in his mid-twenties, has already sold a number of short stories to magazines and anthologies and has begun a career in television scripting. He shows promise of making a strong mark of his own. Their combined tal-ents concentrate here on the claustrophobic aspects of terror.*

H_{e awoke.}

It was dark and cold. Silent.

I'm thirsty, he thought. He yawned and sat up; fell back with a cry of pain. He'd hit his head on something. He rubbed at the pulsing tissue of his brow, feeling the ache spread back to his hairline.

Slowly, he began to sit up again but hit his head once more. He was jammed between the mattress and something overhead. He raised his hands to feel it. It was soft and pliable, its texture yielding beneath the push of his fingers. He felt along its surface. It extended as far as he could reach. He swallowed anxiously and shivered.

What in God's name was it?

He began to roll to his left and stopped with a gasp. The surface was blocking him there, as well. He reached to his right and his heart beat faster. It was on the other side, as well. He was surrounded on four sides. His heart compressed like a smashed soft-drink can, the blood spurting a hundred times faster.

Within seconds, he sensed that he was dressed. He felt trousers, a coat, a shirt and tie, a belt. There were shoes on his feet.

He slid his right hand to his trouser pocket and reached in. He palmed a cold, metal square and pulled his hand from the pocket, bringing it to his face. Fingers trembling, he hinged the top open and spun the wheel with his thumb. A few sparks glinted but no flame. Another turn and it lit.

He looked down at the orange cast of his body and shivered again. In the light of the flame, he could see all around himself.

He wanted to scream at what he saw.

He was in a casket.

He dropped the lighter and the flame striped the air with a yellow tracer before going out. He was in total darkness, once more. He could see nothing. All he heard was his terrified breathing as it lurched forward, jumping from his throat.

How long had he been here? Minutes? Hours? Days?

His hopes lunged at the possibility of a nightmare; that he was only dreaming, his sleeping mind caught in some kind of twisted vision. But he knew it wasn't so. He knew, horribly enough, exactly what had happened.

They had put him in the one place he was terrified of. The one place he had made the fatal mistake of speaking about to them. They couldn't have selected a better torture. Not if they'd thought about it for a hundred years.

God, did they loathe him that much? To do *this* to him.

Where There's a Will

He started shaking helplessly, then caught himself. He wouldn't let them do it. Take his life and his business all at once? No, goddamn them, *no!*

He searched hurriedly for the lighter. That was their mistake, he thought. Stupid bastards. They'd probably thought it was a final, fitting irony: A gold-engraved thank you for making the corporation what it was. On the lighter were the words: *To Charlie/Where there's a Will…*

"Right," he muttered. He'd beat the lousy sons of bitches. They weren't going to murder him and steal the business he owned and built. There *was* a will.

His.

He closed his fingers around the lighter and, holding it with a white-knuckled fist, lifted it above the heaving of his chest. The wheel ground against the flint as he spun it back with his thumb. The flame caught and he quieted his breathing as he surveyed what space he had in the coffin.

Only inches on all four sides.

How much air could there be in so small a space, he wondered? He clicked off the lighter. Don't burn it up, he told himself. Work in the dark.

Immediately, his hands shot up and he tried to push the lid up. He pressed as hard as he could, his forearms straining. The lid remained fixed. He closed both hands into tightly balled fists and pounded them against the lid until he was coated with perspiration, his hair moist.

He reached down to his left-trouser pocket and pulled out a chain with two keys attached. They had placed those with him, too. *Stupid bastards.* Did they really think he'd be so terrified he couldn't *think*? Another amusing joke on their part. A way to lock up his life completely. He wouldn't need the keys to his car and to the office again so why not put them in the casket with him?

Wrong, he thought. He *would* use them again.

Bringing the keys above his face, he began to pick at the lining with the sharp edge of one key. He tore through the threads and began to rip apart the lining. He pulled at it with the fingers until it popped free from its fastenings. Working quickly, he pulled at the downy stuffing, tugging it free and placing it at his sides. He tried not to breathe too hard. The air had to be preserved.

He flicked on the lighter and looking at the cleared area, above, knocked against it with the knuckles of his free hand. He sighed with relief. It was oak not metal. Another mistake on their part. He smiled with contempt. It was easy to see why he had always been so far ahead of them.

"Stupid bastards," he muttered, as he stared at the thick wood. Gripping the keys together firmly, he began to dig their serrated edges against the oak. The flame of the lighter shook as he watched small pieces of the lid being chewed off by the gouging of the keys. Fragment after fragment fell. The lighter kept going out and he had to spin the flint over and over, repeating each move, until his hands felt numb. Fearing that he would use up the air, he turned the light off again, and continued to chisel at the wood, splinters of it falling on his neck and chin.

His arm began to ache.

He was losing strength. Wood no longer coming off as steadily. He laid the keys on his chest and flicked on the lighter again. He could see only a tattered path of wood where he had dug but it was only inches long. It's not enough, he thought. It's not enough.

He slumped and took a deep breath, stopping halfway through. The air was thinning. He reached up and pounded against the lid.

"Open this thing, goddammit," he shouted, the veins in his neck rising beneath the skin. *"Open this thing and let me out!"*

I'll die if I don't do something more, he thought.

Where There's a Will

They'll win.

His face began to tighten. He had never given up before. Never. And they weren't going to win. There was no way to stop him once he made up his mind.

He'd show those bastards what willpower was.

Quickly, he took the lighter in his right hand and turned the wheel several times. The flame rose like a streamer, fluttering back and forth before his eyes. Steadying his left arm with his right, he held the flame to the casket wood and began to scorch the ripped grain.

He breathed in short, shallow breaths, smelling the butane and wool odor as it filled the casket. The lid started to speckle with tiny sparks as he ran the flame along the gouge. He held it to one spot for several moments then slid it to another spot. The wood made faint crackling sounds.

Suddenly, a flame formed on the surface of the wood. He coughed as the burning oak began to produce grey pulpy smoke. The air in the casket continued to thin and he felt his lungs working harder. What air was available tasted like gummy smoke, as if he were lying in a horizontal smokestack. He felt as though he might faint and his body began to lose feeling.

Desperately, he struggled to remove his shirt, ripping several of the buttons off. He tore away part of the shirt and wrapped it around his right hand and wrist. A section of the lid was beginning to char and had become brittle. He slammed his swathed fist and forearm against the smoking wood and it crumbled down on him, glowing embers falling on his face and neck. His arms scrambled frantically to slap them out. Several burned his chest and palms and he cried out in pain.

Now a portion of the lid had become a glowing skeleton of wood, the heating radiating downward at his face. He squirmed away from it, turning his head to avoid the falling pieces of wood. The casket was filled with smoke and he could breathe only the choking, burning smell of it. He coughed his throat hot and raw. Fine-powder ash filled his mouth and nose and he pounded at the lid with his wrapped fist. Come on, he thought. Come on.

"Come on!" he screamed.

The section of lid gave suddenly and fell around him. He slapped at his face, neck and chest but the hot particles sizzled on his skin and he had to bear the pain as he tried to smother them.

The embers began to darken, one by one and now he smelled something new and strange. He searched for the lighter at his side, found it, and flicked it on.

He shuddered at what he saw.

Moist, root laden soil packed firmly overhead.

Reaching up, he ran his fingers across it. In the flickering light, he saw burrowing insects and the whiteness of earthworms, dangling inches from his face. He drew down as far as he could, pulling his face from their wriggling movements.

Unexpectedly, one of the larva pulled free and dropped. It fell to his face and its jelly-like casing stuck to his upper lip. His mind erupted with revulsion and he thrust both hands upward, digging at the soil. He shook his head wildly as the larva were thrown off. He continued to dig, the dirt falling in on him. It poured into his nose and he could barely breathe. It stuck to his lips and slipped into his mouth. He closed his eyes tightly but he could feel it clumping on the lids. He held his breath as he pistoned his hands upward and forward like a maniacal digging machine. He eased his body up, a little at a time, letting the dirt collect under him. His lungs were laboring, hungry for air. He didn't dare open his eyes. His fingers became raw from digging, nails bent backward on several fingers, breaking off. He couldn't even feel the pain or the running blood but knew the dirt was being stained by its flow. The pain in his arms and lungs grew worse with each passing second until shearing agony filled his body. He continued to press himself upward, pulling his feet and knees closer to his chest. He began to wrestle himself into a kind of spasmed crouch, hands above his head, upper arms gathered around his face. He clawed fiercely at the dirt which gave way with each shoveling gouge of his fingers. Keep going, he told himself. *Keep going*. He refused to lose control. Refused to stop and die in the earth. He bit down hard, his teeth nearly breaking from the tension of his jaws. *Keep going*, he thought. *Keep going!* He pushed up harder and harder, dirt cascading over his body, gathering in his hair and on his shoulders. Filth surrounded him. His lungs felt ready to burst. It seemed like minutes since he'd taken a breath. He wanted to scream from his need for air but couldn't. His fingernails began to sting and throb, exposed cuticles and nerves rubbing against the granules of dirt. His mouth opened in pain and was filled with dirt, covering his tongue and gathering in his throat. His gag reflex jumped and he began retching, vomit and dirt mixing as it exploded from his mouth. His head began to empty of life as he felt himself breathing in more dirt, dying of asphyxiation. The clogging dirt began to fill his air passages, the beat of his heart doubled. *I'm losing!* he thought in anguish.

Suddenly, one finger thrust up through the crust of earth. Unthinkingly, he moved his hand like a trowel and drove it through to the surface. Now, his arms went crazy, pulling and punching at the dirt until an opening expanded. He kept thrashing at the opening, his entire system glutted with dirt. His chest felt as if it would tear down the middle.

Then his arms were poking themselves out of the grave and within several seconds he had managed to pull his upper body from the ground. He kept pulling, hooking his shredded fingers into the earth and sliding his legs from the hole. They yanked out and he lay on the ground completely, trying to fill his lungs with gulps of air. But no air could get through the dirt which had collected in his windpipe and mouth. He writhed on the ground, turning on his back and side until he'd finally raised himself to a forward kneel and began hacking phlegm-covered mud from his air passages. Black saliva ran down his chin as he continued to throw up violently, dirt falling from his mouth to the ground. When most of it was out he began to gasp, as oxygen rushed into his body, cool air filling his body with life.

I've *won*, he thought. I've beaten the bastards, *beaten* them! He began to laugh in victorious rage until his eyes pried open and he looked around, rubbing at his blood-covered lids. He heard the sound of traffic and blinding lights glared at him. They crisscrossed on his face, rushing at him from left and right. He winced, struck dumb by their glare, then realized where he was.

The cemetery by the highway.

Cars and trucks roared back and forth, tires humming. He breathed a sigh at being near life again; near movement and people. A grunting smile raised his lips.

Looking to his right, he saw a gas-station sign high on a metal pole several hundred yards up the highway.

Struggling to his feet, he ran.

As he did, he made a plan. He would go to the station, wash up in the rest room, then borrow a dime and call for a limo from the company to come and get him. No. Better a cab. That way he could fool those sons of bitches. Catch them by surprise. They undoubtedly assume he was long gone by now. Well, he had beat them. He knew it as he picked up the pace of his run. Nobody could stop you when you really wanted something, he told himself, glancing back in the direction of the grave he had just escaped.

Where There's a Will

He ran into the station from the back and made his way to the bathroom. He didn't want anyone to see his dirtied, bloodied state.

There was a pay phone in the bathroom and he locked the door before plowing into his pocket for change. He found two pennies and a quarter and deposited the silver coin, they'd even provided him with money, he thought; the stupid bastards.

He dialed his wife.

She answered and screamed when he told her what had happened. She screamed and screamed. What a hideous joke she said. Whoever was doing this was making a hideous joke. She hung up before he could stop her. He dropped the phone and turned to face the bathroom mirror.

He couldn't even scream. He could only stare in silence.

Staring back at him was a face that was missing sections of flesh. Its skin was grey, and withered yellow bone showed through.

The he remembered what else his wife had said and began to weep. His shock began to turn to hopeless fatalism.

It had been over seven months, she'd said.

Seven months.

He looked at himself in the mirror again, and realized there was nowhere he could go.

And, somehow all he could think about was the engraving on his lighter.

Getting Together

The telephone rang. She answered it.

"Hello?" she said.

"Gladys?"

"Milton?"

"Yes," her husband answered. "Gladys, darling, I'm afraid I won't be able to make it home for dinner tonight."

"Oh, my dear. You're working late at the bank again?"

"No." She thought she heard him swallow. "I've been arrested, Gladys."

"*Arrested*!" Her brown eyes widened.

"Oh, it's just a silly mistake, darling," he soothed. "Nothing at all to worry about."

"But, why did they arrest you, sweetheart?"

"Well, it seems that I resemble some thug who killed a rich old lady for her money last night, darling."

"But that's *absurd*!" she cried. "Lover."

"I know it, dearest," he said, "but, well you see, I have no proof to the contrary, darling. While this terrible deed was being committed, I was in the neighborhood, walking to the subway."

"But that's absurd!" she cried.

"I know it, darling," he said apologetically, "but well you see, there are witnesses who claim that I'm the man.

"But that's..." Her hands began to tremble. "Oh, Milton sweet," she said, "what are we to *do*?"

"Well," he said, "if you could get a lawyer for me, dear."

"Yes," she said, "I'll get one right away. Now don't you fret, lover. Everything will be all right."

"Of course," he said. "Yes, of course it will be, Gladys darling."

Unfortunately, it wasn't.

The situation degenerated into a flagrant miscarriage of justice, a gross outrage of law, and a dirty shame. On purely circumstantial evidence, Milton Freef was found guilty of pushing that china closet on top of that old lady and making off with her savings.

"...at which time you will be executed in the electric chair," the judge intoned his final intonation.

At which, Gladys Freef slipped off her chair into a dead heap, taking down with her the lawyer's papers, bifocals, and homburg.

"Oh, my dear," she murmured to her glassy-eyed husband in the prison visiting room some days later. "I can't go on without you. I'll simply *die*."

"Courage," he squeaked. "Perhaps the lawyer's appeal will turn the tide."

"Oh, Milton, lover," she said passionately. "It must. It simply *must*."

Getting Together

It didn't. And the man who really pushed that china closet on top of that old lady blew all the stolen money on a huge drinking party at a lush hotel, during which he bet he could hop along a terrace railing on one foot and lost. As the terrace was on the fortieth floor, the loss was irreparable.

A distraught Gladys Freef purchased a gun.

Religious scruples restrained her from suicide. Therefore, venturing forth into the street, she shot the first passerby, an Albert Somerset of 1911 Albermarle Road, Brooklyn, New York, in the head.

She was picked up, tried, and found guilty of murder in the first degree despite her lawyer's plea of insanity.

She was allowed to visit with Milton in a special visiting room, where both visitor and visited were prisoners.

"Oh dearest, you shouldn't have done it," Milton said, grasping feebly at her hand.

"I had to, sweetheart," she replied, the love light shining in her eyes. "Now we'll be together."

They both sighed, were permitted a kiss, and then were led away. A sentimental judge set Gladys's execution for the same day as Milton's.

Three days later, however, a certain Rockwell Asbury, of the bank where Milton had worked, returned from a two-week vacation and, upon hearing about the situation, went immediately to the nearest police station.

"Yes," he said, "on the night that old lady was murdered, I walked a half block behind Milton Freef all the way to the subway."

"Why didn't you tell us about this before?" they asked him peevishly, and he reiterated that he'd been on a vacation since the night in question fishing for trout in Quebec, although he hadn't caught anything but a bad cold in the head.

Milton Freef was exonerated and released. He visited Gladys with a heavy heart.

"Gladys," he said hollowly. "My love."

"Oh, my darling," she said, trembling wholly. "Now I shall die alone. "Oh, how *cruel* it is!"

Milton held her shaking hand in what, for him was a steely grip.

"Don't despair, Gladys, my dearest," he muttered through clenched teeth. "I won't desert you now. We'll be together, don't you fret."

Whereupon, that evening, he purchased a pistol at a downtown pawnshop and, emulating Gladys, went out on the street and fired at the first passerby, a Miss Marilynne Francescatti of Queens, missed, fired again, and made it. When the police car came, Milton Freef was waiting cheerfully.

There was another trial, during which Milton's lawyer pleaded insanity but with no more success than had Gladys's attorney. He was found guilty of murder in the first degree and, since a date had already been set for his execution, it was restored intact.

They met in that special room again and held fond hands.

"Oh, honey lover," she said, "you did it for me."

"Yes," he replied huskily. "Now we'll be together, darling."

They were led away to their separate cells, both content, both resigned.

Until two days later when the appeal formerly filed by Gladys's lawyer was granted and her sentence of death was altered to a sentence of confinement in the state insane asylum.

Her outraged objections were interpreted as signs of mental breakdown, and she was removed from prison in a straight jacket, screaming and kicking.

Getting Together

Milton, upon being informed of this twist of fate, fell into a state of acute melancholia, during which he sought feverishly for an answer to this cruel dilemma.

The following morning, when the guards brought breakfast to prisoner Freef, they found him unclothed on all fours, attempting to climb the wall of his cell and baying.

The prison psychiatrist was notified and, for several days, observed Milton with a suspicious eye, being an old hand at this sort of thing.

It wasn't until Milton began butting his head against walls that the psychiatrist decided that something was genuinely wrong. Where upon, after lengthy investigation, during which the lie detector revealed that prisoner Freef was telling the truth when he said he was Cosmo de Medici, the psychiatrist, reluctantly, pronounced him insane and, regretfully, recommended his removal to the state insane asylum.

At last! Milton Freef rejoiced within at the thought that he would be together with his beloved Gladys again. He put up only token resistance as they swathed him in straight jacket and led him away.

When he reached the asylum, however, he learned that, two days previous, Gladys had finally proved, to the satisfaction of the staff, that she was not insane after all. She had left the asylum early that morning, singing happily because she believed she was going to join her dear husband.

Milton, upon discovering this, fell into such a violent state that his protestations of sanity went unregarded. He was put into a special cell, padded, to brood.

There, cannily, he evolved a plan for escape. He knew he could not bear to live without Gladys. Therefore, he would break out of the asylum, go to the prison on the day of her execution, demand entrance, be shot down, and thus join Gladys in the bourne beyond.

Two weeks and a day later, a docile Milton Freef was allowed to walk the grounds with his keeper. While strolling behind a hydrangia bush, Milton, who had read of such things in his youth, pressed a vital nerve on the burly keeper's neck and rendered him unconscious. Then, scaling the high brick wall, Milton ran quickly down the highway.

In a farmhouse a few miles down the road, Milton stole a raincoat and returned to the highway. There, in answer to his beckoning thumb, a car stopped.

"You would like a ride?" said the kind old lady in the car.

"I would like your car," said Milton and, as gently as he could, dragged her off the front seat and threw her in a ditch.

He then began the long drive to the state penitentiary. He did eighty all afternoon long, his heart singing a happy song about returning to his love.

About ten that night, however, Milton Freed began to get sleepy. Several times, his head nodded, each time jerking up with enforced alertness, dark eyes shining angrily. He *would* get back to Gladys!

But, at eleven, his head slumped over fatally, and the car rode across the center line.

Just before the black limousine came roaring out of the night, Milton looked up in confounded horror, blinded by the glaring headlights.

"Oh *no*!" he cried.

Then the crash. An awful crash.

Milton Freef crawled, dying, from the rubble of the old lady's car which was, luckily for the old lady, insured.

"Gladys," he moaned horribly, "*Gladys*."

"*Milton*."

He thought he dreamed or was losing his mind.

"What?" he murmured, "What?"

But then, crawling from the twisted wreckage of the limousine came Gladys.

Getting Together

They inched toward each other, glazed eyes shining with love.

"Gladys. Is it really *you*, my precious?"

"Yes, lover! I...convinced them...I was insane—again. They were taking me back."

They met. Their hands touched.

"Together," sighed Gladys in happy agony. "Oh, dearest."

"At last," sobbed Milton. "My sweet."

Whereupon they kissed, both of them expiring in glorious expiration.

The tall man looked at them with sympathy. He sighed. I'm afraid my hands are tied," he said. "After all—*murder*." He clucked and shook his head. "We'll have to keep you separated. Perhaps, after a century or two, we might reconsider." Shrugging, he scratched his right horn. "*Mal chance*," he said.

He smiled. "Good try, though," he added.

Person to Person

T he ringing telephone stirred Millman from his sleep. His eyelids fluttered as he drifted up toward consciousness. The telephone kept ringing and he groaned. "All right, all right."

Sliding his left arm from beneath the covers, he reached to the bedside table, feeling for the handset. His fingers closed around it and he carried the receiver to his ear. "Yes?" he mumbled.

He listened to the dial tone for a few seconds before grimacing irritably and reaching out to thump the handset back on its cradle.

His eyes opened wide as he looked toward the bedside table.

The telephone was still ringing.

He stretched out his arm and fumbled for the lamp switch. Twisting it, he averted his face from the glare, then picked up the handset again and pressed the receiver to his ear.

There was only the dial tone.

Millman stared, bewildered, at the handset. He could still hear the sound of a telephone ringing.

Several moments passed before it came to him that the ringing was inside his head.

~~~~~~~~~

"I have the test results," Dr. Vance told him.

Millman waited anxiously. "My immediate assumption was that it was *tinnitus*," Dr. Vance continued. "There's no sign of middle-ear infection, though, no symptoms such as earache, fever, a sensation of pressure in your ears."

"What *is* it then?" Millman asked.

"You know for a fact it doesn't ring all the time."

"Only at night," Millman answered. "It wakes me up."

"That wouldn't be the case if it was *tinnitus*," Dr. Vance said. "The ringing would be constant."

Millman looked at him in worried silence.

"Don't tell anyone I said this," Dr. Vance went on, "but you might try getting a chiropractic adjustment on your neck. I had a friend who suffered from what appeared to be *tinnitus*. After he got a neck adjustment, it went away."

"And if that doesn't work?" Millman asked.

"Try it first," the doctor said.

~~~~~~~~~

Millman twisted on the bed with an angry groan.

The telephone was ringing again.

He reached out quickly with his left hand and grabbed the handset, carrying the earpiece to his head.

Person to Person

Then he slammed the handset down on its cradle. "Damn!" he cried.

He lay on his back, a look of apprehension on his face as he listened to the sound of the ringing telephone inside his head.

~~~~~~~~~

"Everything's been tried?" Dr. Palmer asked.

"*Yes*," Millman said despairingly. "There's no sign of a fracture or a concussion. Nothing wrong with my spine. No sign of any foreign body. No growths, no tumors, *nothing*. I even had a neck adjustment. It made no difference."

"The ringing happens every night?" Dr. Palmer asked.

"Yes."

"At the same time?"

"Three in morning," Millman answered. "I can't sleep any more. I just lie in bed waiting for it to start."

"And you're positive it sounds like a telephone ringing."

"It *is* a telephone ringing," Millman said impatiently

"Try answering it then," suggested Dr. Palmer.

~~~~~~~~~

Millman lay on his back in the darkness, listening to the ringing sound inside his head. He wanted desperately to make it stop. But Dr. Palmer's suggestion disturbed him. It seemed a bizarre thing for a therapist to say.

Still...

The telephone kept ringing. Millman's left hand twitched as though about to reach for the telephone on the bedside table. But he knew that wasn't where the ringing was coming from.

Impulsively, he visualized a telephone inside his head. He visualized his left hand picking up the handset. "Hel-*lo*," he said aloud.

"Well, finally," said the voice.

~~~~~~~~~

Millman felt himself recoil into the mattress, heartbeat pounding suddenly. "*My God*," he said.

"Take it easy now," the voice responded, that of a man. "Don't get yourself in an uproar. There's a simple explanation."

Millman couldn't seem to breathe.

"Still there?" the man's voice asked.

Millman swallowed. He sucked in a wheezing breath and muttered, "Yes."

The voice said, "Good."

Millman had to ask, although he knew it was insane. "Who *is* this?" he said.

"The name's not important," the man's voice replied. "I'm not allowed to tell you anyway."

"What are you talking about?" Millman's voice strained.

"Take it *easy*," the man's voice said. "You're getting yourself upset for nothing. I told you there's a simple explanation."

"*What*?" demanded Millman.

"Okay," the man's voice answered. "Here's what's going on. It's a government project; a *secret* project, it goes without saying. You'll have to keep it quiet. It's a matter of national security."

Millman's mouth slipped open. *National Security*?

"I won't go into background," the man's voice continued. "You know the situation in the world. Our government maintains a constant policy of espionage. We have to know what's happening on the other side."

Person to Person

"But—" Millman started.

"Just listen," the man's voice interrupted. "We have agents all around the globe, sending us information. The transmission of their messages has always been a risk. Any device they use can be detected sooner or later. Which is why we're experimenting with inner-brain communication."

"*Inner-brain—?*"

"Yes." The man's voice cut Millman off. "A method by which agents can transmit information with no risk whatever of being intercepted. I don't mean telepathy or anything like that. I'm talking about a microscopic insert."

Millman tightened. "*What?*"

"*Relax*," the man's voice told him. "If it's so minute it never even showed up on your medical tests, it's certainly too small to bother you."

Millman tried to speak but couldn't.

"You're probably wondering why you were chosen for this experiment," the man's voice continued. "Actually, you're not the only one. I can't tell you how many there are, but the number is considerable. As to *how* you were chosen, it was mathematical; a random generator."

"*I don't understand*," Millman said.

"To be perfectly candid," the man's voice went on, "only a few of you have reached the stage of answering our call. The rest are still fixated at the point of thinking it's a physical affliction, making endless rounds of doctor visits. Congratulations on being imaginative enough to answer the ringing—it *is* that of an actual telephone, by the way."

Millman braced himself. "But—" he began.

"—we never asked," the man's voice finished Millman's thought. "True. And we're sorry it disturbed you. Still—under the circumstances, we couldn't very well have asked for your permission.

"At any rate," he added, "we won't be bothering you as much now. The connection's been made."

"*For how long*?" Millman asked.

"I'm sorry," the man's voice responded. "That's not my decision to make."

Inside his head, Millman heard the distinct sound of a telephone handset being placed on its cradle.

He fell back on the pillow; he'd been unaware that he was leaning on his right elbow throughout his conversation with the man. In spite of his distress, he felt relieved that the ringing noise had stopped.

In seconds, he was heavily asleep.

~~~~~~~~~~

The ringing of the telephone inside his head jarred Millman awake. His eyes sprang open and he twitched on the mattress. "*No*," he said. It had been five days since he'd spoken with the man. He'd begun to hope it was over; that either the calls would not continue or that he'd imagined everything.

Grimacing, he snatched up the unseen handset. "*Yes*," he said.

The ringing continued.

Millman looked confused. He visualized the telephone as clearly as he could, lifted the handset and brought it to his ear. "Hel-*lo*," he said.

The telephone kept ringing. Was it because he hadn't heard it for the past five nights that it sounded so painfully shrill to him?

In his mind, he visualized his hand grabbing at the handset. "Hello!" he said.

The ringing didn't stop. Millman made a pained noise. The sound seemed to pulse in stabbing waves against the tissues of his brain. He clenched his teeth, face contorted.

Person to Person

The telephone kept ringing. Millman kept snatching up the handset in his imagination, crying out, "Hel-*lo*!"

Abruptly, then, the man's voice answered. "You don't have to *shout*."

"For God's sake!" Millman cried.

"Take it *easy*," the man's voice told him.

"*Easy*?" Millman said. "The phone's been ringing in my head for ten minutes straight!"

"Five," the man corrected.

"Well, *why*?" demanded Millman.

"I've been *busy*." The man's voice had an edge to it. "You're not the only line I have to deal with, you know."

"I'm *sorry*," Millman said in a shaking voice. "But you—" He broke off, frowning. "Why did you keep *ringing* me then?"

"Oh, was I ringing you? I didn't realize," the man's voice said.

Millman looked astonished as he heard a handset click down in his head, breaking the connection.

Seconds later, the telephone began to ring again.

No matter how often he answered it, there was no response.

The ringing continued almost until dawn, Millman lying wide-eyed on his bed, teeth clenched, hands like talons clutching at the sheets.

~~~~~~~~~~

"I was wondering what happened to you," Dr. Palmer said.

Millman drew in labored breath. "I thought I knew what it was," he said. "I thought I had to keep it quiet."

"Keep what quiet?" Dr. Palmer asked.

When Millman had finished telling him what happened, Dr. Palmer gazed at him without acknowledgment.

Millman swallowed nervously. "I'm still not sure I'm not making a mistake in telling you," he said, unable to endure the silence. "But he's driving me crazy, ringing me every night from three a.m. to six and never answering."

Dr. Palmer began to speak, hesitated, then finally said, "You believe this?"

Millman regarded him blankly.

"You believe it's a secret government project?" the therapist asked.

"Well—" Millman broke off in confusion. "That's what he *said*. He—"

The expression on Dr. Palmer's face stopped him.

"David," the therapist said. "Does it really make sense to you?"

Millman struggled for an answer. "I—" He stopped; braced himself. "I *hear* the telephone ringing," he said. "I *answer* it. The man's voice *speaks* to me. I'm not imagining it."

Dr. Palmer sighed. "David, think about it," he said. "A secret government project? Citizens picked at random? Microscopic telephones implanted in their brains without them knowing it? Espionage agents of the United States government transmitting information this way?" He looked at Millman challengingly.

Millman stared back, feeling a heavy weight on his back. Dear God, he thought.

He fought against the feeling. "But I *hear* the ringing," he insisted. "I *hear* the man's voice."

"David, not to alarm you," Dr. Palmer replied, "but hearing voices in one's head has been in the symptomatology tradition for a long time."

~~~~~~~~~

Millman drank black coffee with supper that evening. He wanted to remain alert.

Person to Person

Lying on his bed in the dark, propped on pillows leaned against the headboard, he waited for the ringing of the telephone to start.

And thought about what Dr. Palmer had said.

He'd gotten angry at the therapist's remark about hearing voices in one's head. Was Dr. Palmer implying that he'd gone insane?

"Not at all," the therapist had reassured him. "What I'm saying is that you're undergoing some kind of mental constraint. That your mind is seeking out a method of redressing it."

"By dreaming up a phone call from some secret government project?" Millman had responded tensely.

"The means by which the human mind attempts to deal with hidden problems can be infinite," Dr. Palmer had told him.

The room was still. Millman heard the whirring of the electric alarm clock on the bedside table.

Was Palmer right? he wondered.

True, it did seem awfully farfetched that the national government would go to such lengths to conduct a project so outlandish.

Still, the alternative…

Millman bared his teeth in anger. It was all irrelevant anyway. If the man's voice didn't answer any more—and it hadn't in a week—what difference did it make? Palmer might be convinced that presently the voice would speak to him again because it needed to, but he was certainly not—

Millman caught his breath, jerking back against the headboard as the telephone began to ring. His gaze jumped to the clock. It was three.

He let the ringing go on for thirty seconds before mentally picking up the handset and saying, "Yes?"

"*We're very displeased with you*," the man's voice said; Millman tensed at the tone of it. "You were asked not to say anything about the project, weren't you?"

Millman swallowed nervously.

"*Weren't* you?" the man's voice snapped.

"Yes, but—"

"You were told it was a matter of national security," the man's voice cut him off. "Yet still you told your therapist."

Millman couldn't seem to fill his lungs with air. He made a wheezing sound. "How do you know?" he asked, his voice frail and breathless.

"Figure it out," the man's voice said. "If we can hear your voice when you speak to *us*..."

He didn't finish. Millman shuddered. *Every word*? he thought in dismay. *Every single word I say*?

He struggled to resist. "You know what he told me then," he said. "You know what he thinks you are."

"*Sure*," the man's voice answered scornfully. "I'm not Agent 25409-J. I'm not William J. Lonsdale. I'm not married with three children. I don't work for the C.I.A. I'm your goddamn subconscious mind. Jesus, Millman. What the hell's the matter with you?"

Millman had no answer. He lay immobile, staring up into the darkness. He thought he heard the breathing of the man on the other end of the line.

"All right, listen to me," the man's voice said then. "We're going to try to cut you off the circuit. We *have* been trying for a week now; that's why we haven't spoken to you. I'll put it on priority now that you've blabbed to your therapist about us. Jesus, Millman!"

Millman heard the sound of a handset being set down.

Hard.

~~~~~~~~~~

"But don't you *see*?" Palmer said with a smile. "Your subconscious mind was reacting angrily to having its ruse exposed. A step forward, David."

Person to Person

"He said he was going to cut me off the circuit."

Dr. Palmer shook his head, still smiling. "He won't cut you off," he said. "He has things to say."

What if I don't want to listen to him anymore?" Millman said.

"David" Dr. Palmer said. "*David*. Cons*ider*. You're being given an invaluable opportunity: to engage in dialogue with your own subconscious mind."

"What if the voice keeps picking on me? Millman asked.

The therapist's gesture was casual.

"Hang up on him," he said.

~~~~~~~~~

When the telephone began to ring in his head, Millman was loathe to answer it. The resonating jangle of the bell set his teeth on edge. Even so, it was preferable to the man's potentially abusive voice.

He remained immobile on the bed, a flinching expression on his face.

Could he hang up on the man?

Further, could he snatch up the invisible handset after the connection had been broken, making it impossible for the man to call him anymore? He imagined hearing a dial tone in his head, then an operator's voice, breaking in to tell him he should hang up if he wanted to make a call.

Millman scowled. Now he really *was* beginning to think like a man who was losing his mind.

Abruptly, he picked up the imaginary handset and said, "Hello."

"Thank you for answering," the man's voice said.

Millman tightened. *Now what*? he thought.

"I apologize for speaking out of turn during our last conversation," the man's voice said. "It was uncalled for."

"*Yes, it was*," Millman said impulsively.

"I'm sorry," the man replied. Before Millman could respond, he continued. "Listen," he said, "I'm going to level with you."

Millman's eyes narrowed. *Now* what? he wondered.

"This government project thing," the voice went on. "It's all a lie."

Without thinking, Millman drew his left hand near his face to stare at it as though he actually held a handset in his grip.

"There's no such thing," the man confessed. "Your Dr. Palmer was correct. It *doesn't* make sense. Microscopic telephones implanted secretly in people's brains? I can't believe you bought it."

Millman made a sound of spluttering exasperation.

"I'll tell you what it is," the man's voice said. "I won't give you my name because I'm afraid you might report me to the police. They'd lock me up and throw the key away if they found out what I'm doing."

"What are you talking about *now*?" Millman demanded furiously.

"I'm an inventor," the man's voice said. "I've developed an apparatus which radiates short-wave energy that penetrates the mind of anyone the beamer is directed at, enabling two-way conversation with them. You're the first."

Millman couldn't tell if he felt horrified or enraged. The clashing emotions kept him speechless.

"I know this is as hard to believe as the government project idea," the man's voice continued. "The government would love to get their hands on this, I guarantee you. I'd destroy it first though. It gives me the creeps thinking what our government would do with this device. I'd never—"

Millman broke in fiercely. "*Why are you doing this to me*?" he demanded.

"As I said," the man's voice answered patiently, "I chose you as my first subject. I didn't have the nerve to tell you what was really going on so I made up the story about a government project when all the time—"

It all burst out explosively from Millman. "*Bull-shit!*" he snarled. "I don't believe this story any more than I believe the other! You're no inventor" My therapist's been right all the time! You're my own—"

"You *fool!*" the man's voice cut him off. "You god-damned fool!"

Millman tried to answer but the words choked in his throat.

"You just can't leave well enough alone, can you?" the man's voice criticized him. "Just can't let me do this my own way. No! Not you! You're too goddamned smart for that!"

The animal-like sound the man made drowned out Millman's faint reply. "Well, you're *not* smart! Not at all!" the man's voice cried. "You're *dumb!* You always *have* been dumb! A dumb boy and a stupid man! Davie, you're an *idiot!*"

Millman lurched in shock as the handset crashed down in his head.

He lay in silence, struggling for breath.

He knew the voice.

~~~~~~~~~

Dr. Palmer gazed at him without a word.

Millman drew in a laboring breath. "I have to tell you something about my family," he said. "Something I never told you before."

"Yes?" asked Dr. Palmer.

"My mother suffered from dissociated consciousness," Millman said. "I mean, she was psychic. I won't go into details but she proved it many times."

"Yes?" Dr. Palmer's tone was still noncommittal.

"I think I inherited her ability," Millman told him.

The therapist had difficulty repressing a look of aggravation. "You're suggesting—" he began.

"I'm *telling*," Millman broke in irritably. "You were *right*. It's not a secret government project and it's certainly not what the man's voice told me last night."

"Instead—" Dr. Palmer prodded.

"It's my father," Millman answered.

The therapist didn't reply. He rubbed his lowered eyelids with the thumb and forefinger of his left hand. Millman felt a tightening of resentment in his body.

Dr. Palmer opened his eyes. "You believe that he's communicating with you from 'the other side' as it were?" he asked.

Millman nodded, features hardening. "I *do*."

The therapist sighed.

"Very well," he said. "Let's talk about it."

~~~~~~~~~~

The instant the telephone rang in his head, Millman snatched up the imagined handset. "I'm here," he said.

"That was prompt," the man's voice replied.

"I know who you are," Millman told him.

"You do." Millman had a fleeting impression of his father's face, a smile of faint amusement on it.

"Yes, I do," Millman answered. "Father."

The man chuckled. "So you've caught me," he said.

Millman was unable to control a throat-catching sob. "*Why are you doing this*?" he asked.

"*Why*?" the voice responded incredulously. "Why do I want to speak to my only begotten son? You ask such a question, *Davie*? Is it so difficult to comprehend?"

Millman was crying now. Tears ran off the sides of his face, soaking into the pillow case. "*Pop*," he murmured.

"I want you to listen to me now," his father's voice continued.

Millman's chest hitched as he sobbed.

"Are you listening?" his father's voice inquired.

"Yes." Millman rubbed the trembling fingertips of his right hand over his eyes.

"The reason I'm calling you," his father's voice went on, "is that I feel you should be cognizant of certain things."

"What things?" Millman asked.

"You don't know?" his father's voice responded.

"No," Millman sniffled, rubbing a finger underneath his dripping nostrils.

His father's sigh was deep. "I'll have to tell you then," he said.

Millman waited.

"You're a loser," his father's voice told him.

"*What*?" asked Millman.

"I have to *explain*?" said his father's voice. "You leave me *nothing*? All right; I'll lay it on the line then. You married a bitch. You let her bleed you dry in every way. You let her poison the minds of your two sons against you. You let her divorce proceeding take you to the cleaners. You let her rip away your *manhood*.

"On top of that, you're a loser at your job. You let that moron boss of yours kick you around like a ball. You scrape to him and let him treat you like a piece of dog shit. *Dog shit*, Davie! Don't bother to deny! You know it's true! You're a loser in every department of life and you *know* it!"

Millman felt as though paralysis had gripped him, body and mind.

"*Can you deny a single word I've spoken*?" his father's voice challenged.

Millman sobbed. "Pop," he murmured pleadingly.

"Don't Pop me, you goddamn loser!" his father's voice lashed back. "I'm ashamed to call you my son! Thank God I'm dead and don't have to see you getting kicked around day after day!"

Millman cried out, agonized. "Pop, *don't*!"

~~~~~~~~~

Dr. Palmer rose from his chair and walked to the window. He had never done that before and Millman watched him uneasily, dabbing at his reddened eyes with a tear-clotted handkerchief. The therapist stood with his back to Millman, looking out at the street.

After a while, he returned to his chair and sat down with a tired grunt. He gazed at Millman silently. What kind of gaze was it? Millman wondered. Compassionate? Or fed up?

"I don't do this ordinarily," Dr. Palmer began. "You know my method: to let you find the answers yourself. However—"

He exhaled heavily and clasped his hands beneath his chin. "I feel as though I simply can't allow this to proceed the way it's going," he continued. "I have to say something to you. I have to say—" he winced "—*enough*, David."

Millman stared at the therapist.

"I do not believe—any more than I believe it was a secret government project or an isolated inventor—that your father is communicating with you from beyond the grave. I believe, as I have from the start, that your subconscious mind has, somehow, found a way to speak to you *audibly*. Trying to establish some kind of resolution to your mental problems."

"But it's *his voice*," Millman insisted.

"David," Dr. Palmer's voice was firm now. "You believed it was the voice of Secret Agent 25409-J. You then believed, albeit briefly, that it was the voice of some inventor. Can't you see that this subconscious voice of yours *can make itself sound like anyone it chooses*?"

David felt helpless. He knew he couldn't bear any more of the abuse his father's voice had heaped on him. At the same time, he felt sick about the possibility of losing touch with his father.

"What should I do?" he asked in a feeble voice.

"*Confront it*," Dr. Palmer urged. "Stop just listening and suffering and *talk back*. Start *retaliating*. Demand answers; explanations. Speak *up* for yourself. It's *your* subconscious, David. Hear it out but don't permit it to harass you mercilessly. *Take control*."

Millman felt exhausted. "If only I could sleep," he murmured.

"That I can give you something for," the therapist said.

~~~~~~~~~

He couldn't confront the voice that night. He did as Dr. Palmer prescribed and took two capsules, sleeping deeply and without remembrance. If the telephone rang in his head, he didn't hear it.

It relaxed him enough to enjoy a good night's rest. At work the following day, he even found Mr. Fitch endurable. Once, he almost spoke back to him but managed to repress the impulse. There was no point in losing his job on top of everything else.

During the evening, Millman thought about Elaine and the boys.

Had the voice—whoever it belonged to—spoken the truth? *Was* Elaine a bitch who'd poisoned the minds of his sons against him? Was that why their behavior, when they saw him, was so remote? He'd told himself it was because they got together so infrequently; that he was virtually a stranger to them.

What if it was more than that?

It *was* true that the divorce settlement had left him very little. Still, it had been *his* choice. He didn't have to give her so much.

Thinking of it all made Millman tense and edgy, ready to confront the voice.

At three a.m., when the ringing in his head began, he grabbed the unseen handset and yanked it to his head. "I'm here," he said.

"*Are* you, Davie?" his father's voice responded scornfully.

"You can cut it out now," Millman answered.

"Cut what out, little boy?" his father's voice inquired mockingly.

Millman braced himself. It took all the will he had to resist that voice which had intimidated him throughout his childhood and adolescence.

"You're not my father," he said.

Silence.

Then his father's voice said, "I'm not?"

"No, you're not," Millman said, trying to keep his voice strong.

"Who *am* I then?" his father's voice asked. "The King of Siam?"

Millman shuddered with uncertain anger. "*I don't know*," he admitted. "I only know you're not my father."

"You're a stupid boy," his father's voice responded. "You've always been a stupid boy."

"I defy you!" Millman cut him off. "*You're not my father!*"

"Who *am* I then?" the voice demanded.

"Me!" cried Millman. "My subconscious mind!"

"Your *subconscious mind*?" The voice broke into sudden laughter; totally insane, the laughter of a maniac.

"Stop it," Millman said.

Person to Person

The laughing continued, uncontrolled, deranged. Millman visualized a face behind it—white and twisted, staring, wild-eyed.

"*Stop* it," he ordered.

The laughter rose in pitch and volume. It began to echo in his head.

He had to mentally slam down the handset three times before the laughter cut off.

His hands almost vibrating they shook so badly, he washed down a pair of capsules.

When the telephone began to ring inside his head again, he tried to ignore it, waiting tensely for the drug to lower him into a heavy, deafened sleep.

~~~~~~~~~

The tiny, black-haired woman opened the door to her apartment and looked at Millman questioningly. She didn't look as old as he knew her to be.

"I spoke to you on the telephone this afternoon," he said. "I'm Myra Millman's son."

"Ah, yes." Mrs. Danning's false teeth showed in a smile as she stepped back to admit him.

There was a smell of burning incense in the dimly lit living room. Millman noticed crosses and religious paintings on the walls while he moved to the chair the tiny woman pointed at. He sat down, hoping that he wasn't making a mistake. Momentarily, he imagined Dr. Palmer's reaction to this. The idea made his throat feel dry.

Mrs. Danning perched on a chair across from him and asked him to repeat his story.

Millman told her everything from its beginning to the manic laughter. Mrs. Danning nodded when he spoke about the laughter. "That may well provide the clue," she declared. He wondered what she meant by that.

He watched in anxious silence as she closed her eyes and began to draw in deep, laboring breaths, both hands on her lap, palms facing upward.

Several minutes later, her features hardened with a look of disdain. "So," she said. "Now you see a psychic." Mrs. Danning bared her teeth so much that Millman saw her pale gums. "You just won't listen, will you?" she said. "You have to keep investigating. *Asshole!*"

Millman twitched on his chair, eyes fixed on the psychic. She had begun to rock back and forth, a humming in her throat. "Oh, yes," she said after a while. "Oh, yes." She repeated the words so many times that Millman lost count of them.

After ten minutes, she opened her eyes and looked at Millman. He began to speak but she raised her right hand to prevent it. He waited as she picked up a glass of water from the table beside her chair and gulped down every drop of it. She sighed.

"I think we have it now," she said.

~~~~~~~~~

"For God's sake, David!" Dr. Palmer cried. Millman had never heard such disapproval in the therapist's voice.

"I wasn't going to come back," he said defensively. "Wasn't going to tell you. But I thought you might be sympathetic."

"To what this woman told you?" Dr. Palmer asked, appalled. "That you're being possessed by some— some—?" He gestured angrily.

"*Earthbound spirit*," Millman said, willfully. "A disincarnate soul held prisoner by the magnetism of the living, doing everything he can to—"

"David, David." Dr. Palmer looked exasperated and despairing at the same time. "We're losing ground. Every time we get together, we seem to fall back a little more."

"*The spirit is not at peace*." Millman's voice was stubbornly insistent. "It wants to experience life again. So it invades my mind—"

"David—!" the therapist cut him off. "*Please!*"

Millman pushed up from his chair. "Oh, what's the use?" he muttered.

"Sit down," Dr. Palmer told him. Millman stood before the chair, unable to decide.

"Please sit down," the therapist requested quietly.

Millman didn't move at first. Then he sat back down, a look of sullen accusation on his face. "I don't think you appreciate—" he began.

"I appreciate that you are going through one hell of an ordeal," Dr. Palmer broke in.

"But you don't believe a word I've said."

"David, use your head," the therapist replied. "*Did you really think I would?*"

Millman blew out tired breath.

"I suppose not," he conceded.

~~~~~~~~~

He had never in his life felt so divided in his mind—so torn between desire and dread.

On the one hand, he wanted the telephone to ring in his head so he could resolve this madness.

On the other hand, he was terror-stricken by what might happen if he answered it.

Easy enough for Palmer to repeat his conviction that it was his subconscious mind.

What if he was wrong?

Millman was thinking that for what might well have been the hundredth time when the telephone began to ring in his head.

He drew in a long, slow, chest-expanding breath of air, then let it out until his lungs felt empty. All right, he told himself.

The time had come.

He saw the handset in his mind. Saw his left hand pick it up. Almost felt the earpiece press against his head. "*Yes*," he said aloud.

"This is your father," the voice replied.

Millman answered, "No."

"What did you say?" The image of his father's face appeared in Millman's mind: thin-lipped, critical.

"*You're not my father*," he said.

"Who am I then?"

"*I don't know*," Millman answered desolately. "I just know you're not my father." Amazingly, he *did* know it now.

"You're right," the man's voice told him.

Millman started. *Was this the beginning of some new ploy*? he wondered. "Who *are* you then?" he demanded.

"This is a secret government project and I'm Agent 25409-J—" the man's voice started.

"Stop it," Millman said through clenched teeth. "Don't start that again. I won't have it."

"I'm an inventor," said the voice. "I've created a device that—"

"*Stop* it," Millman cut him off.

"Right," the man's voice said. "This is your father."

"*Stop* it, damn it!" Millman cried.

"Correct," the man's voice said. "I'm an earthbound spirit possessing you."

"God damn it, that's enough!" Millman shouted. He felt his heartbeat pound.

"*Right*," the man's voice said. "This is Krol. I'm speaking to you from the planet Mars."

"I'm hanging up," Millman said.

He imagined doing it.

"You can't hang up," the voice informed him. "It's too late for that."

Millman stiffened. "Yes, I can," he said. He tried again to put the handset down.

"I'm *telling* you," the voice said coldly. "You can't *do* it anymore."

Millman made a frightened sound and tried again.

"You *should* be frightened," said the voice. "I'm going to kill you now."

Millman's body spasmed with a shudder. He slammed the handset down on its invisible cradle.

"I'm going to kill you now," the voice repeated.

"Get away from me," said Millman.

"Not so." The man's voice was one of cruel amusement. "You're mine now, little porker. Don't you know who this really is?"

"*Get away from me*," Millman's voice was trembling now.

"All right, I'll tell you who I am," the man's voice said. "I have many names. One of them is Prince of Liars. Isn't that a gas?"

Millman shook his head, teeth gritted hard. Again and again, he slammed down the unseen handset.

"You're wasting time, little porker," said the man's voice. "I'm in charge now. Want to hear some other names? Lord of Vermin. Prince of Sinners. Serpent. Goat. Old Nick. Old *Davy*! Isn't *that* a gas?!"

"Get away from me!" cried Millman. "I won't listen to you anymore!"

"Yes you will!" the voice cried back. "You're mine now and I'm going to kill you!" The maniacal laughter began again.

Millman reached for the vial of capsules.

"That won't do you any good," the man's voice told him gleefully. "You can't escape me now."

Millman didn't try to answer. Shaking uncontrollably, he picked the cap off, shaking two capsules onto his palm.

"*Two*?" the man's voice asked. "Not half enough, old man. You'll never get away from me. You're mine, I'm going to kill you dead."

The laughter started in again, booming in some cavern in his mind.

Millman washed a pair of capsules down his throat, water spilling across his chin.

"Not half enough!" the man's voice cried, exultantly. He continued laughing with demented joy.

Millman pressed another capsule in his mouth, another, washed them down.

"*Not half enough*!" the man's voice yelled at him. "*You've let me in too long*!"

Millman's palsied hand shoved capsules in his mouth. He washed them down. The glass was empty now. He gulped down capsules dry, his face a mask of terror.

"Secret government project!" howled the voice. "Inventor! Father! Earthbound spirit! Krol from Mars! The Devil! Take another capsule, David!"

Millman lay on his right side on the bed, legs drawn up, twitching. *God, please take me out of here*! he kept begging, sobbing helplessly.

"*Your wish is my command*," the voice said finally.

~~~~~~~~~

Inside his head, the telephone began to ring.

He lay in his bed, hands clasped behind his head, grinning at the sound.

Then he chuckled, picking up the handset in his mind. "Y*e*-es," he said musically.

"Please," the man's voice said.

"Please?" he said as though he didn't understand. "Please what?"

"*Please let me back*."

"Oh, no," he chided. "After all the trouble I went to? Keeping you so occupied you never dreamed what was coming? After all that work, you want me to let you *back*?"

His face became a mask of feral animosity.

"*Never*, asshole," he said. "You are out of here for good."

"No!" the man's voice cried.

He snickered. "Gotta go now, babe," he said.

He put the handset down, giggling as he visualized the look of shock on Davie's face. The little shit would try again of course, he knew.

While he waited for the ringing to begin, he made his plans for tomorrow.

First, a call to Elaine. Not another fucking nickel, bitch. And tell that pair of cretins you dropped not to bother me again.

As for Fitch—his eyes lit up—what sheer delight it was going to be to smash that ugly bastard in the mouth and stalk out on that nowhere job.

Then off to enjoy himself. Travel. Women. Fun. Women.

He'd worry about money when he ran out of it.

As for Palmer—he laughed aloud—the clever son of a bitch had it right all the time.

Now let him try to collect his bill!

He was cackling at the idea when the telephone began to ring in his head.

With a hissing smirk, he reached into his mind and yanked out all the wires. The ringing stopped abruptly. There, he thought.

He wouldn't need that line any more.

CU: Mannix

While Mannix waited for the receiver to be lifted on the other end of the line, he gazed at the back of his right hand. It was a trim, powerful hand, the skin darkly tanned, the nails immaculately manicured. He spread the fingers and drew them hard into a fist. A good hand, strong and healthy-looking, not a sign of age.

His legs twitched as the intermittent buzzing in the earpiece broke off with a click. "Good afternoon, Renken-Blasker," said the girl's voice.

"Dale Mannix, dear," he told her. "Burt in?"

"*Yes*, Mr. Mannix—right away." Her tone was properly reverential. Mannix smiled and drew in slowly on his stomach muscles, glancing downward. His chest was spare and nut-brown. Hard, he thought. Who says I'm sixty-two? I'll flatten him.

"What can I do for you, Dale?" Burt Renken's voice inquired.

"Just got a new phone," Mannix told him. "Called to give you the number."

"Shoot," said Renken.

Mannix looked at the receiver. "276-5090," he read.

"Got it," Renken answered. "Old number out the window?"

"No, no—just wanted a second one, exclusively for business." He was briefly, pleasantly conscious of his voice—its warmth and variations.

As he hung up, Mannix stared across the wide expanse of lawn toward the pool. Inger was rubbing tanning lotion over her nude, tawny form. Mannix shivered as she squirted oil drops across her breasts and rubbed them lingeringly into the skin. He thought of going out there in the sun with her. In his imagination, he could feel the soft, hot moistness of her skin.

He made a grumbling sound and picked the script back up. Have to learn these bloody lines, he told himself. He propped the handtooled-leather binder on his lap and tried to concentrate. He'd never been too good at reading, though. Not that he didn't have a memory he'd match against the best. No one—but no one—had a better grasp of dialogue than he did. It was the reading itself that bored him. All that damned descriptive garbage.

Mannix crossed his muscular legs and cleared his throat, his eyes on the poolside chaise again. Inger was on her stomach now. She stretched out, resting her head on her arms. What was she thinking of? he wondered. *Who* was she thinking of?

Flexion in his neck again. Trapezius, he thought. He clenched his teeth, visualizing tension spasms in the damaged muscle. He stared out at her naked form. To look inside that golden head, he thought—to see, to *know*.

He glanced at the telephone suddenly, the idea sprung to full bloom in his mind. Smiling, he picked up the receiver and dialed their old number. Fortunately,

CU: Mannix

Maria was out shopping. He started as he heard the jangling of the telephone in the entry hall. To be on both ends of the line at once was an odd sensation. He couldn't hear the poolside telephone.

He smiled as Inger reached out lazily for the receiver. It made him feel godlike to realize that he knew everything and she knew nothing about that ringing telephone beside her.

She lifted the receiver. "Hello?" she said.

That voice—he shivered at the sound of it. Casually, he reached across the table by his leather chair, removed a tissue from its dispenser, folded it in quarters, and held it over the mouthpiece. "Hel*lo*," he replied.

"Who's this?" asked Inger.

"Don't you know?" he asked. His famous blue-grey eyes were crinkling at the corners. He could see them as he had so many times – in close-up, on wide-screen, in Technicolor.

"No," she said. Interest or impatience? Mannix lost his smile. He couldn't tell.

"Let's just say a fond admirer."

Inger murmured. "Oh?"

Ice water running up the backs of his legs. It wasn't impatience. "Come on, you know," he said.

"I don't," she protested—mildly.

Mannix turned his head, releasing shaky breath. She knew, he told himself. She was putting him on, that's all. "Sure you do," he insisted. He felt that internationally famous knot of vein at his right temple starting to pulse. "Take a guess."

"How can I?" she asked.

Mannix fumbled on the chairside table, feeling for his eyeglasses. "Try," he said impulsively. "We've met, you know." He realized abruptly that his voice was that of Gresham, the sly Chicago lawyer in *Point of Order*, Universal, 1958. His agent had told him he was crazy to do that one, that it would hurt his image.

"Met where?" she was asking.

"One of those parties," he answered.

He had the glasses now. He slid them hastily across his ears and nose bridge. Inger sprang into focus. "What do you look like?" she asked him.

You'd better know it's me, he thought. The planes of his face were hardened now—that look of threatening anger movie audiences knew the world over: woe betide his enemies now. He looked out coldly at her, his neck beginning to stiffen. "If I told you what I look like," he said, "you'd know who I am and the game would be over."

He covered the mouthpiece, sucked in breath. Hell, let it go, a voice suggested. *No*, he answered. He'd suspected this for some time now. Let it come out.

"All right," she said, "let's see."

He waited.

"You're—fifty. No, no—sixty," she said.

Mannix grinned. You knew all along, you Kostlich kraut, he thought, delighted. He closed his eyes abruptly, trying not to recognize the surge of gratified relief that filled him. "That old," he heard himself say.

"I'm only teasing," she said.

Mannix opened his eyes.

"You're under forty, I imagine," Inger said.

"That's right," Mannix felt his heartbeat, slow and heavy. "Thirty-eight to be exact." He stared out through the window. Inger had her left arm pressed beneath her breasts, nudging them upward. "That's not old at all," she said.

She *didn't* know. Mannix felt ill. "No, it isn't old," he said with Gresham's voice. "I'm still completely capable of—" (beat): he saw it written on a script page "—quite a bit."

He felt his flesh grow cold as Inger's soft laugh drifted from the earpiece. "I'll *bet* you are," she said.

CU: Mannix

Mannix blinked. His head felt light. "I *am*," he told her. "Interested?"

He shuddered as she slid her feet back on the chaise, pushing up her knees. Her legs remained together for an instant, they slumped sideways and apart. "Why should I be interested in you?" she asked.

Mannix felt the pulsing at his temple quicken. Her tone, her posture. *She was willing*.

He twitched as Inger sat up, turned around, and looked back toward the study window. She *did* know! Mannix felt his heartbeat jolt. He waited for her smile, her wave, some sign of recognition. He deserved her mockery for this. He'd take it gracefully and—

Mannix felt himself go numb as Inger turned back and reclined once more. "Well?" she asked.

"Well, what?" She had to recognize his voice now— he wasn't even trying. But he had to try! Abruptly, he was back inside the other man. "Why should you be interested in me? Because I'm good in bed. Damn good." Please, he thought. Please tell me that you know it's me.

"Are you really?" Inger said.

Mannix shivered violently. "If I was there I'd show you."

That laugh again. He'd fought the realization for a long time, but he knew it now: it was an obscene laugh. *Inger* was obscene. "If you were here," she said, "you'd *have* to show me because I'm lying in the sun without a stitch on."

He stared out through the window at her. Now her legs were far apart, her left hand was back behind her head. She's ready for you, Mister, Mannix thought.

The swimming pool reflected like a mirror in the moonlight. Mannix stared at it. Bel Air was soundless at this time of night. He heard a bird chirp somewhere in the darkness.

He turned and looked at Inger.

Her body was stretched out on the bed like some sleek, well fed animal. She *is* an animal, he thought. Less than half an hour before she'd straddled him with panting fierceness. "*Köstlich! Köstlich!*" (Delicious! Delicious!) Who had she really straddled in the darkness though? (She had turned the lamp off, not he.) That man who phoned her this afternoon? He hadn't seen her so excited in a year.

Mannix walked across the carpeting and stood beside the bed, gazed down at the golden flood of hair across the pillow, at her browned, voluptuous figure.

All through dinner he had waited for the laughter. They'd gone over to The Swiss House—she doted on Viennese cooking. They'd gotten one of the tables in back and, as they'd eaten, he'd kept waiting for the laughter to begin—for her to tell him how ridiculous he was. At one point, when he'd seen her smiling to herself, he'd asked her what was funny—felt his hands begin to shake with final hopeful readiness.

"Nothing," she had said. He'd stared at her and known that everything he'd feared for all these years was true: he was that most despised and ludicrous of men— the cuckold.

Mannix leaned over tremblingly and pulled out the drawer of his bedside table. Reaching in, he drew out his pistol and pointed it at Inger.

No. He shook his head. Ruin his career for her? He smiled contemptuously at her slack Germanic features. Thirty-seven years he'd been a star. He'd be insane to end that for a moment's dubious revenge. He put the pistol back into the drawer.

He took off his robe and lay down on the bed beside her. Now that he'd made up his mind to divorce her, he was amused at himself for having thought, even for a moment, that she was clever enough to have fooled him.

CU: Mannix

He clucked. Too bad, he thought. Marriage number four gone down the tube. Amusing that, for the first time, it was not because of *his* unfaithfulness. The public would never believe it, of course. Not that they should—the other enhanced his image better. Mr. Romance. He winced. What idiot columnist had made that up?

It was good all morning. Makeup at six, shooting at seven. The scenes were long and his. There were a lot of takes without excessive waits for setups. With what spare time there was, he entertained the cast with anecdotes about the Golden Years—memories laced with humor, charm, and wit. He did it beautifully. To lure and hold with words—to be "on" before a rapt, attentive audience—there was nothing like it. It was almost sensual.

Then it was over and he was in his dressing room. Lunch was called. He wasn't hungry. He sat inside the lavish trailer, staring at the telephone. How long had she been cheating on him? In the almost three years of their marriage, how many times?

Mannix jerked the telephone receiver off its cradle and dialed his home number. As if it were someone else's hand, he watched it draw the neatly pressed and folded handkerchief from the pocket of his grey slacks and press it down across the mouthpiece. Now what? asked his mind. You're dumping her. Isn't that enough?

It's not, he thought.

"Mannix residence," said Maria.

Mannix cleared his throat, "Mrs. Mannix, please."

"One moment," said Maria.

As he waited, Mannix wondered where she was. She could still be in bed. She liked to sleep late after making love. Love? he thought. He'd never manage to associate that word with her again.

She picked up an extension. "Yes?"

Mannix licked his lips. "Hel-*lo*," he said.

189

"Who's this?"

"You know who it is," he answered.

"Do I?"

Mannix tensed. "Sleep well?"

"I always sleep well," Inger answered.

Yes, you do, he thought—you aren't bright enough to suffer from anxiety.

She yawned. "Look, I have to go unless—"

Mannix cut her off. "Meet me," he said. He knew it was absurd, and yet he smiled with mirthless pleasure at the thought.

"Oh, I couldn't do that," she protested.

Her coyness made his stomach turn. "Tomorrow," Mannix told her. He could almost see her. She was sprawled across the bed, still naked.

"What makes you think I want to meet you?" she asked.

"Because you'd love it," he answered. His fingers clamped in on the bridge of the receiver. "You and me in bed, like animals."

It was almost anti-climactic when she murmured, "Where?"

The dressing room was blurred around him, swimming. Mannix felt like very heavy, very fragile glass. If he moved, he'd shatter. "Beverly Hills Hotel," he said. It sounded like a first reading. "Three o'clock tomorrow afternoon."

She's going to do it, he thought. He couldn't seem to breathe.

"How will I know you?" Inger asked.

The answer spun immediately to mind. "Just ask for Mr. Smith's room," Mannix said, "Eddie Smith."

"I don't know an Eddie Smith." She sounded suddenly confused.

"Real names tomorrow, baby," Mannix answered.

"Oh, I see," said Inger.

CU: Mannix

No, you don't, he thought, you don't see anything, you stupid bitch.

"Will it be fun?" she asked. He saw her face quite clearly now. The edges of her teeth were set together, eager and excited.

Mannix answered. "You have no idea."

He'd yet to take the first sip of his Pimm's Cup. He was sitting in a corner of the Polo Lounge, stirring with its slice of cucumber while he stared at the key on the table. The plastic tag was face up: 315. Eddie Smith's room, Mannix thought. A faint smile drew his lips back. Right, he thought.

Some men walked across the lounge and waved to him. He didn't wave back. He had no desire to talk to anyone. He really should have chosen some more remote spot. Everybody knew him here. Still, what difference did it make? He wasn't here to murder her—just to see a look of stupid bafflement across her face.

Mannix had to smile. It was rather funny, actually—the idea of this Eddie Smith. Mannix saw him as a college football player gone to lard, maybe a small-time actor making out with women who set their standards at the minimum level: any stud in a storm.

Smith could resemble that one over there: broad shoulders, curly blond hair, tight clothes—the jacket a shade too loud, the low-grade silk shirt. Sub-par all the way.

He blinked. The blond young man was smiling at him. Mannix tensed, about to cut him off, when the idea came—instantly complete, completely beautiful. Mannix smiled broadly. How much more satisfying than a look of bafflement on Inger's face. He gestured for the young man to come over.

The young man stood with obvious delight and as he crossed the lounge Mannix realized abruptly that he *was* an actor—he had seen him somewhere in some undistinguished role performed with undistinguished flatness. Mannix almost chuckled. The young man would perform all right, he thought; through any indicated hoop. He'd have to—it was part and parcel of his hunger to succeed. They were all the same.

The young man stopped in front of him. "Good afternoon, Mr. Mannix," he said. His smile was that of all young, struggling actors, Mannix thought, straining for unwonted charm—too bright, too many teeth displayed.

"Sit down," Mannix said.

The young man was unable to restrain a startled grin. "Why, *thank* you," he responded. He sat with lithe dispatch. Lifts weights, thought Mannix. Studies at some one-horse acting school, played a few supporting roles in non-pay theater groups, has a list of TV credits adding up to zero. "What's your name?" he asked, his voice genial, interested.

The young man swallowed. "Jeff Cornell," he said sincerely. Who made that up? Mannix wondered. Probably some agent. "Cornell," he tasted. "Seems to me I've seen you somewhere."

"I just did a part on *L. A. Law*," Cornell supplied immediately.

"Of course," said Mannix. He hadn't seen it. "And very good, too," he added, smiling.

"Why, thank you, Mr. Mannix," said Cornell. "That's very kind of you."

Not exactly, Mannix thought. The young man's dazzling smile amused him. Exactly what he needed. "Tell you what I have in mind," he said. "I need a favor."

"I'll do anything I can, Mr. Mannix," Cornell answered gravely.

I know you will, thought Mannix. Anything at all. "I want you to meet my wife at three o'clock," he said. "I want you to seduce her." Not even Olivier could mask a reaction to that, he thought.

CU: Mannix

It wasn't surprising that Cornell's face went almost completely blank. "Is—?"

"—this a joke?" completed Mannix. "No, it isn't. I have reason to believe that my wife has been unfaithful." With a platoon of different men, the sentence finished in his mind. "I want to divorce her, but I have to have some evidence."

"But—" Cornell looked distressed.

"You have carte blanche," continued Mannix, using the tone of whimsical bittersweetness that had endeared him to a generation of moviegoers. "You can go the distance if you want to. I have every reason to believe she won't object. That part doesn't interest me. My one concern is catching her. You understand?"

He could see that Cornell was trying unsuccessfully to understand.

"Let me give it to you once again," said Mannix. Now his voice had bite. "Number one: I know my wife's been cheating on me. Number two: I need evidence that will stand up in court. Number three: If I can trap her in a compromising state, I'll have that evidence." He leaned back, fingering the key tag. "Not too hard a job," he said. "She won't say no, I guarantee you." He paused for effect. "And in return," he finished, "you acquire a featured part in my next film which commences shooting this fall in London."

He waited, thinking: I can hear the wheels turn. A featured part in Dale Mannix's next film? London in autumn? *The big chance!*

Jeff Cornell would draw and quarter his mother for less.

Mannix checked his wristwatch. It was only three-nineteen. Come *on*, he thought. He drank some Scotch and sat the glass down irritably. What were they doing now? He winced. His neck was stiffening again. Disturbances like this were bad for him. He should be home, relaxing in the sun, not sitting here. *God damn her, anyway!*

He looked at his watch again. Seven minutes more. He drew in trembling breath. Play it cool, he told himself. He'd have it made in seven minutes: the delight of seeing Inger's dazed expression and the evidence he'd need to dump her without cost. As for Cornell—He smiled. London in the fall would not see Jeff Cornell before any cameras. Idiot, Mannix thought coldly.

The scene projected on his mind again. Inger entering the hotel at five to three, heading for the desk. Mannix had been standing where she couldn't see him and observed her talking to the clerk, then smiling as she crossed the lobby toward the elevator. Room 315, he thought. He picked the key from the table and dropped it into his pocket. Cool, he thought. He pushed away the glass, then eyed his watch again. Time to go.

Mannix stood. He dropped a five-dollar bill on the table and left the Polo Lounge. Crossing the side lobby, he ascended a half flight of steps and entered the men's room. There he scrubbed and rinsed his hands. I'm washing my hands of her, he thought, the concept pleasing him.

He stared at his reflection as he carefully combed his black and grey-streaked hair. Sixty-two? he thought. Absurd. He didn't look a day past forty-five. He was lean and hard. To hell with Inger. Who needed her? He was Dale Mannix. He didn't need anyone. He straightened his black knit tie. *Hic jacet*, cunt, he thought, you've had it. Mannix is about to dump you—right into the garbage can where you belong.

The elevator was waiting. He stepped inside and pressed the button. He was Vince DeMaine in *City Heat* going up to kill his faithless wife. No, that was unreality, he thought. This was happening; he was merely getting rid of excess baggage. She could play around on someone else's money. As for him, there were still a lot of numbers in his book.

The doors slid open. Mannix left the elevator, listening to his footsteps. Room 325. He pressed his shoulders back, visualizing himself as he walked: tall, distinguished, on top of the world. Room 323. If Academy Awards were given for true-life performances, he'd win one for the scene he was about to play. 321. He smiled. Let them be naked, he thought. 319. His words were going to hit them with far more impact than bullets. 317. A few more paces.

Mannix stopped outside the room and listened. There was no sound inside. He waited tensely. What were they doing? He reached into his pocket and withdrew the key. Don't let me fumble now! he thought in panic as he almost dropped it. It would be horrible if he unlocked the door so clumsily that she had time to run into the bathroom. They had to be in bed together, naked, staring at him. He would accept no less.

He shoved the key into the lock, twisted it, and pushed the door ajar.

A wave of darkness rushed across him. For a moment, he was certain he was going to faint. His fingers grabbed the doorknob as he wavered.

Jeff Cornell was standing by the window, smoking nervously. Inger was sitting on a chair. Both were dressed. The bed was made.

"*Do* come in," said Inger coldly.

Mannix gaped at her. Her face was pale and rigid, her expression filled with venomous distaste. "Well, are you going to close the door?" she asked. "Or would you rather everyone in the hotel found out about this?"

Mannix pushed the door shut. He felt dazed and numb.

"Disappointed?" Inger asked. "Is your big scene ruined? The outraged husband telling off the guilty wife? Did you rehearse it for a long time?"

Mannix couldn't speak.

"You must think I'm awfully stupid," Inger said.

It hit him then. "You *knew*," he said.

"Brilliant!" she exploded.

"But why—?"

"I have to tell you, don't I?" Inger cut him off. "I really have to tell you—it's impossible for you to understand." She stood up, glaring at him. "I've had it, Dale!" she raged. "Is that clear? Do you understand that? I have *had* it! Years and years of living with your damned suspicions! All right for *you* to have affairs! Oh, yes, of course! *You're* Dale Mannix, you're the big star! Mr. Romance! But *me*? Oh, no, not me! I had to be watched like a criminal! Questioned! Hounded! Constantly suspected! *Well, I've had it, Dale!* This is the last damned straw! Trying to trick me into having an affair with a total stranger so you can trap me with him! You're sick, Dale! *You're sick and you're too damned much for me!*

Mannix reached out feebly. "Inger." He felt cold and sick. "Inger, please." His neck was like a board.

Inger closed the door and locked it, walked across the room, and sat on the bed. Lying down, she gazed up at the ceiling.

That had been the closest one of all. If Cornell hadn't told her what was going on- She shivered, gooseflesh rising on her arms. All that conversation on the phone and she'd never had the least suspicion it was Dale. She groaned. My God, he could have wrapped me up but good, she thought.

She stretched luxuriantly. It was all right now, though. It had worked out perfectly—she might have planned it herself. Dale wouldn't dare suspect her now.

CU: Mannix

Not for a long time, anyway. She laughed softly. It was a riot that the man he'd picked to trap her had gotten her a long reprieve instead.

Inger sighed. And *what* a man, she thought. She was looking forward to spending time with him. She clenched her teeth and murmured, "*Kostlich*."

She turned her head and looked up at the rows of photographs on the wall. Dale Mannix. The big star. Mr. Romance. She snickered. *Old fool*, she thought.

Haircut

Angelo was down the block having lunch at Temple's Cafeteria and Joe was alone, sitting in one of the barber chairs reading the morning paper.

It was hot in the shop. The air seemed heavy with the smell of lotions and tonics and shaving soap There were dark swirls of hair lying on the tiles. In the stillness, a big fly buzzed around in lazy circles. **HEAT WAVE CONTINUES**, Joe read.

He was rubbing at his neck with a handkerchief when the screen door creaked open and shut with a thud. Joe looked across the shop at the man who was moving toward him.

"Yes, sir," Joe said automatically, folding the newspaper and sliding off the black leather of the chair.

As he put the newspaper on one of the wireback chairs along the wall, the man shuffled over to the chair and sat down on it, his hands in the coat pockets of his wrinkled brown gabardine suit. He slumped down in the chair, waiting, as Joe turned around.

"Yes, sir," Joe said again, looking at the man's sallow, dry-skinned face, He took a towel from the glass-floored cabinet. "Like to take your coat off, sir?" he asked, "Pretty hot today."

The man said nothing. Joe's smile faltered for a momen, then returned.

"Yes, sir," he said, tucking the towel under the collar of the mania faded shirt, feeling how dry and cool the man's skin was. He put the striped cloth over the man's coat and pinned it in place.

"Looks like we're havin' another scorcher," he said.

The man was silent. Joe cleared his throat.

"Shave?" he asked.

The man shook his head once.

"Haircut," Joe said and the man nodded slowly.

Joe -licked up the electric shaver and flicked it on. The high-pitched buzzing filled the air.

"Uh...could you sit up a little, sir?" Joe asked.

Without a sound or change of expression, the man pressed his elbows down on the arms of the chair and raised himself a little.

Joe ran the shaver up the man's neck, noticing now white the skin was where the hair had been. The man hadn't been to a barber in a long time; for a haircut anyway.

"Well, it sure looks like the heat ain't plannin' to leave," Joe said.

"Keeps growing," the man said.

"You said it," Joe answered, "Gets hotter and hotter. Like I told the missus the other night..."

As he talked, he kept shaving off the hair on the back of the man's neck. The lank hair fluttered darkly down onto the man's shoulders.

Joe put a different head on the electric shaver and started cutting again.

Haircut

"You want it short?" he asked.

The man nodded slowly and Joe had to draw away the shaver to keep from cutting him.

"It keeps growing," the man said.

Joe chuckled self-consciously. "Ain't it the way?" he said. Then his face grew studious. "Course hair always grows a lot faster in the summertime. It's the heat. Makes the glands work faster or somethin'. Cut it short, I always say."

"Yes," the man said, "short." His voice was flat and without tone.

Joe put down the shaver and pulled the creased handkerchief from his back trouser pocket. He mopped at his brow.

"*Hot*," he said and blew out a heavy breath.

The man said nothing and Joe put away his handkerchief. He picked up the scissors and comb and turned back to the chair. He clicked the scissor blades a few times and started trimming. He grimaced a little as he smelled the man's breath. Bad teeth, he thought.

"And my nails," the man said.

"Beg pardon?" Joe asked.

"They keep growing," the man said.

Joe hesitated a moment, glancing up at the mirror on the opposite wall. The man was staring into his lap.

Joe swallowed and started cutting again. He ran the thin comb through the man's hair and snipped off bunches of it. The dark, dry hair fell down on the striped cloth. Some of it fluttered down to the floor.

"Out?" the man said.

"What's that?" Joe asked.

"My nails," the man answered.

"Oh. No. We ain't got no manicurist," Joe said. He laughed apologetically. "We ain't that high-class."

The man's face didn't change at all and Joe's smile faded.

"You want a manicure, though," he said, "There's a big barber shop up on Atlantic Avena in the bank. They got a manicurist there."

"They keep growing," the man said.

"Yeah," Joe said distractedly, "Uh...you want any off the top?"

"I can't stop it," the man said.

"Huh?" Joe looked across the way again at the reflection of the man's unchanging face. He saw how still the man's eyes were, how sunken.

He went back to his cutting and decided not to talk anymore.

As he cut, the smell kept getting worse. It wasn't the man's breath, Joe decided, it was his body. The man probably hadn't taken a bath in weeks. Joe breathed through gritted teeth. If there's anything I can't stand, he thought.

In a little while, he finished cutting with the scissors and comb. Laying them down on the counter, be took off the striped cloth and shook the dark hair onto the floor.

He rearranged the towel and pinned the striped cloth on again. Then he flicked on the black dispenser and let about an inch and a half of white lather push out onto the palm of his left hand.

He rubbed it into the men's temples and around the ears, his fingers twitching at the cool dryness of the man's flesh. He's *sick*, he thought worriedly, hope to hell it sin 't contagious. Some people just ain't got no consideration at all.

Joe stropped the straight razor, humming nervously to himself while the man eat motionless in the chair.

"Hurry," the man said.

"Yes, sir," Joe said, "right away." He stropped the razor blade once more, then let go of the black strap. It swung down end bumped once against the back of the chair.

Haircut

Joe drew the skin taut and shaved around the man's right ear.

"I should have stayed," the man said.

"Sir?"

The man said nothing. Joe swallowed uneasily and went on shaving, breathing through his mouth in order to avoid the smell which kept getting worse.

"Hurry," the man said.

"Goin' as fast as I can," Joe said, a little irritably.

"I should have stayed."

Joe shivered for some reason. "He finished in a second," he said. The man kept staring at his lap, his body motionless on the chair, his hands still in his coat pockets.

"Why?" the man said.

"What?" Joe asked.

"Does it keep growing?"

Joe looked blank. He glanced at the man's reflection again, feeling something tighten in his stomach. He tried to grin.

"That's life," he said, weakly, and finished up with the shaving as quickly as he could. He wiped off the lather with a clean towel, noticing how starkly white the man's skin was where the hair had been shaved away.

He started automatically for the water bottle to clean off the man's neck and around the ears. Then he stopped himself and turned back. He sprinkled powder on the brush and spread it around the man's neck. The sweetish smell of the clouding powder mixed with the other heavier smell.

"Comb it wet or dry?" Joe asked.

The man didn't answer. Nervously, trying not to breaths anymore than necessary, Joe ran the comb through the man's hair without touching it with his fingers. He parted it on the left side and combed and brushed it back.

Now, for the first time, the man's lifeless eyes raised and he looked into the mirror at himself.

"Yes," he said slowly. "That's better."

With a lethargic movement, he stood up and Joe had to move around the chair to get the towel and the striped cloth off.

"Yes, sir," he said, automatically.

The man started shuffling for the door, his hands still in the side pockets of his coat.

"Hey, wait a minute," Joe said, a surprised look on his face.

The man turned slowly and Joe swallowed as the dark-circled eyes looked at him.

"That's a buck-fifty," he said, nervously.

The man stared at trim with glazed, unblinking eyes. "What?" he said.

"A buck-fifty," Joe said again. "For the cut."

A moment more, the man looked at Joe. Then, slowly, as if he weren't sure he was looking in the right place, the man looked down at his coat pockets.

Slowly, jerkingly, he drew out his hands.

Joe felt himself go rigid. He caught his breath and moved back a step, eyes staring at the man's white hands, at the nails which grew almost an inch past the finger tips.

"But I have no money," the man said as he slowly opened his hands.

Joe didn't even hear the gasp that filled this throat.

He stood there, staring open-mouthed at the black dirt sifting through the man's white fingers.

He stood there, paralyzed, until the man had turned and, with a heavy shuffle, walked to the screen door and left the shop.

Then, he walked numbly to the doorway and out onto the sun-drenched sidewalk.

He stood there for a long time, blank-faced, watching the man hobble slowly across the street and walk up toward Atlantic Avenue and the bank.

An Element Never Forgets

I'm not sure but Leslie J. Boxbishop may have been the greatest physicist that ever lived. I know I will be laughed at for writing this but so was Galileo. I don't care, Leslie J. Boxbishop may not be with us in the flesh but his great daring lives on and I mean to put his memory right. So here is the story.

Leslie and I were room mates at Fort College. We were both majoring in physics but if I was a molehill Leslie was a mountain. He never went out with girls like I did and he only went to the movies once in three years to see Madame Curie in a revival because he didn't believe in radium.

Leslie preferred to stay in our room reading physics books or experimenting with his apparatus. He had no end of equipment from an Allan wrench to a zymometer. Late at night he would still be up, poring over his papers, pressurizing cylinders, separating gold leaves and similar activities. Leslie was always up and doing.

All this is to set the stage for Leslie's great discovery which came like this.

One night in April we were both in the room and Leslie threw his pencil in the air and shouted,

"I have got it!"

I turned to him in surprise.

"What is it?" I asked, "What have you got?"

"Raymond," he said with a fierce light in his eyes. "Raymond, I have just driven the last nail into the coffin!"

"What coffin, Leslie?" I asked him.

"The coffin," he said triumphantly, "In which we shall bury all physics."

"How do you mean?" I asked him.

"Come here," he said, "and I will tell you. I will do better, I will *show* you."

I put down *The Theory of Double Radiometric Isotopes As They Affect Flowers* by J. Woodford and walked over to Leslie. He was squatting on a tripod stool before his apparatus bench. Before him was the sheaf of papers he had been working on for the past two years. Whenever I had asked him what was on them he had winked an eye and said his theory. Was he actually going to reveal it to me now?

"I guess you have been wondering," he said, "What I have written on all these papers."

"Yes," I admitted, "I have." Excited at the thought that Leslie was about to share his secret with me.

"See," he said, "read the title."

I read:

THE THEORY OF THE ELEMENTS
BY
LESLIE J. BOXBISHOP, B.S.

An Element Never Forgets

We were not to graduate for a year and two months yet but I did not cavil about the B.S. I knew he would get one, wild horses couldn't keep him from it. Leslie was straight A.

"Elements?" I said, "Like O and H?"

Leslie pressed his lips together.

"Nonsense!" he said. "How could *that* put all physics in its grave?"

I shrugged and told him I did not know.

"No," he said, in a mystic voice. "No, this is far more than that. My 'Elements' are far more vital and startling."

"What are they?" I asked him.

"What *are* they?" he repeated with the glow of discovery on his face. "Such that no physical law can stand by itself a second more!"

I felt a tremor in my very vitals. Leslie J. Boxbishop, I knew, was not one to make rash claims.

"But," I faltered, "but how can this be? *What is it you have discovered?*"

~~~~~~~~

"What," asked Leslie J. Boxbishop of me, "is one of the very foundations of physical theory?"

"What?" I said, too excited to equate.

"The laws of motion," stated Leslie. "To wit: Every body perseveres in its state of rest or of uniform motion in a straight line unless it is compelled to change that state by forces impressed thereupon."

He paused for emphasis.

"Thus," he said, "the premise that any mass will remain at rest until some external force moves it and that the greater the external force the greater the movement."

"Is this...untrue?" I questioned hesitantly.

"In externals, no!" cried Leslie. "But effect is what we *all* may see, physicist and plumber alike. It is *cause* that is the vital factor!"

"Yes?" My voice failed.

Leslie J. Boxbishop folded his arms.

"I, alone, know the true cause," he said.

"But what…?"

"The Elements," Leslie said simply.

My hands shook.

"But what in God's name *are* the elements?" I cried.

"The Elements," Leslie corrected.

"The Elements," I amended.

"Ah," beamed Leslie, "that is the question."

"The Elements," said Leslie J. Boxbishop, "are submicroscopic beings. Invisible to our eye as," his voice grew harsh. "*Indeed*, are the so-called 'atoms' and 'molecules'."

He glared at me, daring me to refute.

"But, Leslie," I began.

"Theories, theories," he demeaned in angry tones. "I have found *The Truth*!"

He paused to fill his lungs with air.

"To return to the outmoded laws of motion," he said, "which treats mass as some pliant, dead lump which sits, waiting patiently, for some external force to come along and prove Newton's asinine law of inertia."

I stared at him.

"Mass is *not* dead!" he cried, smoting an outraged fist upon his bench. "Mass is a community of Elements, each physical shape its own…*township*, as it were."

He leaned forward, fire in his words.

"When force is applied to mass, these Elements, resentful of intrusion on their natural state of comatose reserve-*move away*! And the faster the external force – the greater the external force—the *faster* and the *greater* will be the movement of escape by the Elements!"

An Element Never Forgets

Leslie looked bitter.

"They do not like our touch," he said solemnly. "And I, for one, do not blame them."

"But Leslie..." I attempted an objection.

"What is it?" he said.

"You say these...Elements are...*alive*?"

"They *are*," he said. "Vitally and functionally alive. As witness their energetic progress in liquid which," he added scornfully, "That *fool* Brown credited to the erratic buffeting of molecules instead of correctly ascribing the movement to the Elements enjoying the swim."

"But if they are sub-microscopic, Leslie," I ventured.

"The moving granules are not the Elements!" Leslie said impatiently, "but merely chaff caught up in the currents created by the swimming Elements!"

"This is incredible," I said.

"Incredible but true," stated Leslie. "There are no molecules, no atoms, electrons nor protons. There are only the Elements."

He paused a second.

"And now," he went on, "with this truth as our premise all phenomena become explicable. The increased pressure and heat in a cylinder as the piston is forced down. Not because of concentrated molecular energy but," he finished, "because the Elements, infuriated and, singularly claustrophobic struggle the more violently to escape."

I gaped at Leslie, unable to speak much less to argue with his astonishing concept.

"To continue," Leslie said. "In all phenomena, great or small, my theory is validated. For an example, take gravity."

"Yes," I said. "Gravity."

"All this talk of attractive forces is so much anachronistic tush," said Leslie. "The case itself is simple to obviousness. As indeed are all the *true* concepts. In short, gravity is no more nor less than the desire of the Elements to have ground beneath them. The fact that all falling objects attain the same rate of speed merely demonstrates that all the Elements, despite differences in attitude and state, have an equal desire for earth's solidity beneath them."

He paused, an ironic twist to his narrow-lipped face.

"And, if for *one moment*," he said, "these minuscules of life decided that they would rather look elsewhere for a home—that, simply, would *be the end of gravity*."

"No!" I cried.

"Yes!" he cried in answer. "Null-g, then, would only be an interplanetary nomadic urge on the part of the Elements."

Silence for a moment as I stared in wonder. Then I said,

"You say there are differences between Elements?" I asked.

"Well, of course!" Leslie said, almost indignantly. "Should they be all the same? Should they not be as fully variegated in idea, impulse and philosophy as man himself?"

"I..."

"Well, of course," said Leslie. "Of course. And is there not *proof* of this truism in physical objectivity? Consider electrostatics, all phenomena of attraction and repulsion. What *are* they but conclusive evidence that the Elements, like anyone else, also have their likes and their dislikes."

He enumerated.

"One," he said, "Physical differences. Greater mass in motion ceased said motion sooner than a lesser mass. Why? Because of friction? Balderdash! Because one community of Elements gets tired sooner than another.

An Element Never Forgets

The larger the community the greater proportion of invalids and young. The larger the increment of fatigue!"

He held up a second finger.

"Two: mental differences. Why do some liquids boil before others, some solids melt before others, some gases ignite before others? Difference in temper, no more nor less. Some Elements are more emotionally unstable than others.

Leslie paused.

"And here," he said, "we come to the crux of the matter. Namely, that man does not realize what he is tampering with!"

He looked grimly at me.

"These Elements never forget! In most experiments I think that, somehow, these Elements realize they are being preyed upon in *ignorance*. And not with deliberate intent. *However*...!"

Leslie flashed a premonitional eye.

"We *can* overdo ourselves," he said, "as in, for a glaring instance, the atomic bombs."

"But how?" I said nervously.

"What is the atomic bomb?" queried Leslie, "but a mass of tortured Elements suffering complete nervous breakdown?"

I shuddered. At the thought.

"The purpose, the *goal* of my pronouncement on the Elements," Leslie expounded, "is a request, nay a *plea* to cease from this hideous mangling of Elements!"

He leaned forward.

"How would you feel?" he asked me, "if some monster entity came along, took your home, melted it to slag and then reformed it into a guided missile?"

I swallowed.

"I should not like it," I said.

"Much less should they like it!" stormed Leslie. "They who were here long before man crawled out of the mud!"

211

Leslie raised a menacing finger.

"We are in danger," he said in a hollow, emotion-spent voice, "if we continue making of this world a *torture-chamber* for the Elements—they will revolt! They do not forget—*poor suffering masses…!*"

At that he fell sobbing on his bed.

I stood there shaken to the core. As his broken sobs scalpeled into my brain I fumbled through his papers, reading from logical beginning to stunning conclusion his theory on the Elements.

Some day I will make them all known.

~~~~~~~~

But not now. Tragic entireties dwarf mere details. As tradition-shattering as those details are.

But I have now to make a terrible revelation. Were I of different caliber I might hide it from the world, preferring rather to let it remember Leslie only as the discoverer of the Elements.

But I must be frank, as unkind as it may seem. For so confident am I of the lasting import of Leslie's discovery that mere personality cannot overshadow it.

That night I tossed fretfully on my pillow unable to sleep, the incredibleness of Leslie's discovery mounting in volume until the very idea threatened to engulf me.

Then morning came somehow and I left Leslie sleeping the sleep of exhaustion. I went to class and spent a restless morning listening to lectures, the content of which remains lost to me to this day.

Then, at noon I returned to our room.

To find poor Leslie—*dead*.

The cause seemed simple, though horrifying enough. Leslie, never the practical thinker, had heated a can of beans without punching air holes. Death from shrapnel had been merciless.

An Element Never Forgets

But that is not the end. How shall I tell it? It tears my heart out yet to reveal the truth.

The truth which I found in the last page of his experiments on the Elements. I quote it verbatim, awful as it is.

I sit here dying. My life ebbs away quickly. I must make this confession. I have fought the horrible realization but I know, at last, that it is too true.

I did it deliberately. I heated the Elements in the can until, driven mad by fear and pain, they combusted and...it is just...killed me.

I am dying. Forgive me, Elements, I have no right to live.

I know you will never forget.

My Conversation with Superman

I know the very title puts you off. I don't blame you. It would put me off as well: That is, it *would* have put me off. Not now. Why? Brace yourself. Think otherwise. *Superman exists*.

What? you say. This fictional aberration? This brainstorm of an over imaginative cartoonist? This bizarre iconic hero figure? *Really exists*? Say on, you insist. Prove it. Well? I can't exactly produce him, flesh and blood. Assuming that he is actually composed of flesh and blood. As we know it, then it means, probably not. But that is part of the answer I have not pursued. Maybe later. That is not my intention at the moment. I simply want to establish one thing – that Superman truly exists. Is not a made-up persona. Exists. For *real*. How do I know? Read on.

~~~~~~~~~~

The contact—if you choose to describe it that way—took place later at night on the downtown express of the B.M.T. subway in Manhattan. My name—if you wish—is Professor Alan Bradbury. Yes, I know. That name rather casts a pall of exaggeration over the entire account. I can't help it. Truth is truth – and all this really took place. Would it be more acceptable if my name was Smith? Jones? Well, let that go. My name is Dr. Alan Bradbury and all this really happened.

It was after one A.M. I'd been attending a faculty meeting at the high school where I teach. Physics, not creative writing if that might be your immediate reaction. I am not the imaginative sort. Give me facts and I flourish. I sup at the table of atomic valves. Just to make sure you don't assume I'm the kind of person who fosters far out notions. Far from it. Let that be established first and foremost. What I'm telling you is absolutely factual. My words are accurate. I swear by them.

One A.M. then. The B.M.T. downtown subway express. The car almost empty. The young man sitting by himself at one end of the car. I dislike crowds myself. So I sat in the same section. The young man glanced up at me, then returned to his thoughts. At least, it seemed to be what he was involved in.

At first, I didn't notice anything specific. Just a rather large young man sitting opposite me. I was mostly absorbed in my current issue of the *New Yorker* magazine.

When I completed reading the article, I gazed across the aisle. To my surprise—and general displeasure—I do not care to be so directly regarded—I saw that the young man was gazing at me. I felt my lips pressing together in critical response. Willfully, I returned to my magazine.

My Conversation with Superman

Shortly thereafter, I allowed my eyes to elevate and observed, to my relief, that the young man was no longer looking at me. Thank goodness for that, I thought. I'd had a momentary apprehension that he might have had kind of amorous interest in me; you know what I mean. Such was not the case, I saw now. Why he had gazed at me so fixedly I would never know. I thought.

At which moment, I became aware of a discrepancy in his appearance.

The upper front of his white shirt had become—or was all the time - unbuttoned. It seemed to me that he had unbuttoned the shirt deliberately and was now about to make some unwarranted gesture. A smile, a wink—God help me!—Some variety of verbal attempt at contact.

Not so. He made no move whatever. As a matter of explanation, I never did discover whether the unbuttoned shirt was deliberate on his part or simply the result of careless dressing. That is hardly the point anyway.

What I *am* stating is, what was—and is, I assume —visible beneath the white shirt. An undershirt, you say? At the very least.

A dark blue shirt—and the upper part of an ornate red letter S.

The poor man is demented, it occurred to me, in the flash of a second. Obviously, it was—is—a shirt identifying the persona of Superman. Now the entire picture fell into place. A young man with some sort of obsession with the man defined as Super. I felt a wash of pity for him. Also a tinge of uneasiness. Was he harmless or should he be institutionalized? At that moment, I had no idea.

I returned, openly, to my magazine reading. If I concentrated on that, maybe the young man would leave me alone. If not, I could get off at the next station and be rid of this awkward situation. This—conceivably—perilous one.

I was re-reading for the third time the opening paragraph of a new article when it happened.

With a loud thump, the young man was sitting next to me. Involuntarily, I looked at him with, I am certain, a measure of distress. He *was* a big man, I noted as though for the first time. His shoulders were uncommonly broad, his chest equally so. Even his hands appeared, to me, to be unusually large. He was wearing a dark, probably black suit and, as I have already mentioned, a white shirt but no tie. Black socks and shoes.

He was gazing at me, I say, curiously—but not exactly that. I can only describe his expression as, let me express it, somewhat *pleading*.

He spoke then. His voice was not a reflection of his impressive girth. It was almost childlike. That sounds strange, I know. But there it was. This veritable colossus of a man had a soft, boy-like voice.

"I'm sorry," he said.

His words confused me utterly. Sorry? For what? I was immediately thrown off balance. "Sorry?" I repeated, making it a question.

"For annoying you," he said.

Annoying me, my mind repeated, still confused.

My Conversation with Superman

"I've never done this sort of thing before," the young man told me. He hesitated.

"No, that isn't true," he contradicted himself. "I tried it once before but had no success."

Now what? I wondered. Explore? Examine the meaning of whatever "this" might be? I simply didn't know.

"I saw you looking at me before," he said.

Oh, no, the reservation instantly ascended in me. Was my original uncertainty correct? Was this entire incident to be reduced to one of sordid import? The possibility made me inwardly cringe. In a state of chilled resistance, I waited for the axe to fall.

It didn't. Instead, the young man reminded me, "You saw my undershirt."

Well, that remark could mean anything. It came to me. Validation of my initial assumption or something else entirely. But what?

"I think you know what it is," the young man said. I could only think of saying, "What?"

"This doesn't mean anything to you?" he asked.

I'm not going to say it, I vowed. If he wants that degree of validation, let him seek it elsewhere. My original estimation was probably accurate. There was probably something amiss in his sanity. It went—

"The S stands for Superman," he informed me.

Well, now it's all on the table, I thought. What was I to do with it? What course should I be taking? Disbelief? Ridicule? I didn't, for a moment, believe that he was Superman. At the same time, to greet his remark with apparent scorn might bring on some sort of retaliatory temper eruption. I was in no mind for that. With an obviously powerful young man? In a virtually empty subway car?

I decided, at that moment, to humor the young man. Otherwise, I might be risking life and limb or at least losing a peaceful subway ride.

"So," I began, "Mister... is it Kent?"

"Rorshak," he replied.

Now I was really stymied. Was his delusion self-defeating? *Rorshak*?

I had to say it. At any rate, I *did* say it. "I thought your name was—"

"—Clark Kent," the young man interrupted. "No. That's the name they've given to me."

Given to me, the words echoed in my brain. *They*? Who were they? In his conviction at any rate.

"No...Clark Kent," I stammered.

"No Clark Kent," he said. "No Lois Lane. No *Daily Planet*. All made up."

"By *who*?" I asked with an edge of aggravation. Was that a mistake on my part? He might still react in a violent manner. I tensed for that.

My Conversation with Superman

It never came. "By the media," was all he said. "The writers. The cartoonists. The movie moguls. All the people who converted—I should say *perverted*—my existence into a money-making enterprise."

Now he sounded too rational. For several moments I almost believed him.

But I couldn't give up. Emboldened by his reasonable demeanor, I continued to probe. "No Lex Luthor, Mister—Rorshak?" I asked. "No...trio of escaped prisoners from your planet? No..." I dropped it. My queries sounded absurd to me.

"None of them," was all he said. "All the creations of others."

"*Well*—" I didn't know how to proceed. What was there left to say?

"You didn't come from another planet?" I risked inquiring. "Your father didn't send you away prior to the planet's explosion?"

"Oh, my father sent me away," he said. "I don't think the planet was in any danger of exploding though. Maybe he just wanted to get rid of me. He was an experimental biologist. Maybe he felt that I was too—how do I put it?—*different*." He made a scornful sound. "As if, on Earth, I'm just a normal human being." He actually chuckled. A dark embittered chuckle. "Mr. Average Man, who can stop a train, carry a ship, possess X-ray vision, jump over a building. Not that I can really jump over buildings. I tried it once and hit the outside of the seventh floor. Luckily, I don't get hurt very easily or at all."

"You can stop bullets too?" I asked. He must have taken note of the disbelieving tenor of my question. Because he didn't respond aloud but only shook his head.

Suddenly, he was gripping my arm. If I had been inclined to accept his account at its face value, that grip alone might have changed my mind. It *hurt. Badly.* When I examined my arm later, it was to see extensive black and blue disfiguration.

He seemed to realize what was happening and abruptly withdrew his hand. "I'm sorry," he said, "I didn't mean to harm you."

"Well, you did," I told him wincing.

"Oh, that was nothing," he said. "If I'd tensed my grip, I'd have broken your arm and crushed your flesh!"

I believed him. For then anyway.

"My apologies," he went on, "I just felt so frustrated because I know you don't believe a word I've said."

My arm still smarting, I countered with some acrimony.

"You're asking me to believe something rather—I mean *very* incredible."

"I know that," he conceded. "I've been living with it for such a long time that, it's a part of my life. Again, I apologize."

"Very well," I told him stiffly. My arm still ached.

My Conversation with Superman

All right then. I'd just go along with his story. *Story*? I thought. Yes. Probably. Beyond comprehension at any rate.

"How *do* you live with it?" I inquired. Let the man speak, I thought. Assume the validity of his words. As difficult as that was. I still felt immersed in the basic incredulity of what he'd told me. But what value was there in voicing my dubious state of mind? Let it go. Easier. It would all be over presently. I thought.

"How do I live with it?" the young man asked. "From day to day. As best I can."

That was the trouble, you see. He made too much sense. If I was Superman, I might say the same thing. I felt another brush of compassion for him. He seemed so desolate, so completely riven of interest in living. Without thinking—only experiencing sympathy for his visible sorrow, I asked him, "How old are you?"

His answer up-ended my entire sense of partial acceptance. "Seventy-six," he told me.

Oh, now here we go again, came the thought. Back to the ridiculous. He looked to be no older than somewhere in his mid-twenties.

"We, apparently, don't age as rapidly where I came from," he explained. I say explained. To me, my arm still in pain, my mind still subject to extreme doubt, his "explanation" seemed, without him realizing it, beyond reason. Insane in fact.

He startled me by saying, then, "I have to get off at the next stop."

Again, without thought, I asked, "You live in this part of town?"

"No. I don't," he answered. "I'm going to my night job."

"Which is—?" I prompted. Why, I don't know.

"Night watchman at a jewelry warehouse," he told me.

I had to ask. As crazy as it was that I was asking at all.

"All these...*feats*," I said. "Did you...actually do any of them?"

"Oh, some," he told me. "A few."

I didn't want him to detail any of them. I knew inherently that I would never believe them anyway.

"You...must be known in some important circles," I said. I know he heard the tone of near derision in my voice.

Whether he did or not—and I'm sure he did—he didn't reply. Instead, he rose with a quick, supple movement; for an instant, the fluidity of his movement almost convinced me again.

"Thank you, Mister—" he began.

"Bradbury," I said. "Doctor Bradbury, PhD," I supplied my identity. Why I went out of my way to make it clear that I was not a medical doctor, I have no idea. Did I think that if he believed me to be a doctor of medicine,

My Conversation with Superman

he might request a physical examination to verify his claim? I didn't know. I still don't. But it's what I did.

"Thank you, Doctor Bradbury," he said. "I appreciate your listening to me. It helped."

I can't imagine why, the thought occurred. It must be obvious to you that I never bought a fragment of your fanciful tale. But be that as it may – I thought I'm always glad to render assistance to a fellow being. That thought brought on an uncontrollable smile and sense of visibility. *Fellow being*? Well, let that go too. No point in dwelling on the situation as unlikely as it was.

Rorshak—what was his first name? I wondered. "S. M." Initials for Superman? That made me smile again. With some regret. The young man did seem in a condition of, almost, despair. I had to sympathize with at least that aspect of the conversation. *Superman*? No. A disturbed individual with a demented fixation? More than conceivable.

The car rolled to a stop and Rorshak—assuming that was really his name—went out. Turning left and heading for the exit, he turned to glance in at me. I looked across my shoulder and saw him raise the fingers of his left hand in what appeared to be a slight parting wave. What I did see distinctly was his final smile. Not much of one but unmistakable in its effect on me. I have to confess that it came close to breaking my heart. For a split second I felt a compulsion to, somehow, run after him. Reassure him that, after all, I believed his incredible story and would do whatever I could as impossible as that inclination was—to assist him. *Assist Superman*? How far-fetched was that compulsion? About as far-fetched as one could imagine, I realized.

Pointless to consider at any rate. He was gone and I was alone with improbable ruminations. So he had a powerful grip. That meant nothing. Body building, weight lifting. Sensible explanations for my aching arm.

The ache diminished in a day or two.

The mania of the problem persisted. Let me explain.

I was in my apartment living room grading mid-term examinations when the doorbell rang.

I fancy I scowled. What idiot could possibly want to see me at—I checked my wrist watch—eleven-forty at night? I remained seated entertaining the hope that whoever it was would depart if I didn't respond to the doorbell.

Which, disappointingly rang again. This time with additional energy. Sighing—or groaning, I forget which, I laid down my pen and examination paper and, standing, trudged to the front door, no doubt muttering, "I'm *coming*, dammit." I opened the door.

Let me be exact about what I saw standing in the hallway.

A man dressed up as a human bat.

Let me repeat that. *A man dressed up as a human bat*. I'm serious. After what I've told you, be advised that I am not brain muddled. All this *happened*. It *did*.

"Doctor Bradbury?" the bat inquired.

What else could I do but nod, somewhat weakly, and say, "Yes?" *Get out*! My mind was screaming. Hadn't I been exposed to enough insanity for one evening?!

My Conversation with Superman

"Al Rorshak suggested that come and see you," said the man dressed as a bat. I couldn't take my eyes off his dark pointy ears. They were very much distracting. None-the-less, my brain was attempting to deal with Superman's first name. *Al*? Superman's first name was *Al*? Now the absolute madness of it all possessed me. I wasn't sure what the bat man had gone on to say but, regardless, I said "What can I do to help you?" I sensed, in a moment, that it was a nonsensical thing to offer. But there it was. It was that kind of night wasn't it? Yes, totally. Beyond question. I was buried in an avalanche of cataclysmic de-mentia and rather than struggle against it with futile result I had best allow it to bury me to the top of my head.

"Al said you had a sympathetic ear," said the bat man. He did, I wondered. I certainly can't tell why. I could only say one word. The work was "So?"

"May I come in?" said the man in the bat suit.

I felt as though I'd lost all ability to resist or con-clude the situation so I merely waved him into my living room.

How do I convey the conspicuous oddity of a man resembling a bat settling down on your sofa? No way, I suspect. Too far gone to elucidate.

"So what's your problem?" I asked. I knew he must have one. Why else would he be there? Why else had Al suggested that he come? *Al*, I thought again, mutely in-credulous. No matter what, I would never be able to think of Superman as *Al*. Not Al. Anything but Al.

I knew that the bat man had spoken but I'd missed his opening words. I was too involved in thought. So, po-litely, I swear, I asked him to repeat what he'd said.

Did I sense a moment of pique on his part? Perhaps. But he re-commenced his speech. Which, I declare with absolute conviction, was as follows.

"I'm in an abyss of difficulties. I'm trapped in this insane predicament. I never, of my own free will, wear this crazy outfit they gave me—*they* again! I'm only wearing it now to convince you of what I'm saying."

"I'm not a man of wealth. I don't reside in a mansion. I don't own a black vehicle with all kinds of power-ridden features, mostly weapons, or a flying machine with similar features. I have no ability to ascend buildings. My name is Jim Wykoff, not Bruce Wayne. And I certainly don't have a butler named Alfred! I'm trapped Doctor Bradbury! *Trapped*! Described by them as possessing all these bizarre accoutrements, all these incredible attributes."

"By *who*?" I asked. Hadn't I presented the same question to Rorshak?

"The same bunch that present similar lies about Mister Rorshak," he told me. Irrelevantly, I felt grateful that he hadn't mentioned *Al* again.

"So...who does all the feats of bravura you get credit for?" I asked.

"Oh, God knows," he said. "All I know is I *do* get credit for them."

So there it is. Take it or leave it. I guarantee that I would be overjoyed to leave it. But I can't. I'm trapped as well.

I'll add this much. The entire time Wykoff—or whatever his name may be—was speaking, I kept wondering how many other friends he had and who they were or believed themselves to be.

A Murder Story Told in Two Hundred Clichés

Ah, you are a heartless wretch!" she cried, throwing herself on the chair with a sickening thud.

The budding genium looked up from his work. Once we were a happy couple, she thought, until he began to get a taste for the almighty dollar, for filthy lucre. She watched his brawny arms move as he sculpted, still looking at her.

This is the last straw, he thought, that I should be fettered to this clinging vine. Oh, for the single blessedness again without benefit of blushing bride now pasty-faced and boring.

A breathless silence hung over them as he moved his hoary head back and looked upon his work again. This is the psychological moment, she thought, ever since the gala occasion last night when the museum directors spread a festive board that made the senses reel—

the dinner in honor of Roger's one-man show. Ever since then she'd been waiting with bated breath for the coup-de-grace she knew would come in one fell swoop. As fast as my legs could carry me then, she thought, I'd run from him.

But, as luck would have it, the argument was conspicuous by its absence. It made her nervous to anticipate it and then not have it occur. Ever since going to bed the night before and lying in the arms of Morpheus, then waking from the briny deep of slumber to hear the feathered songsters trill their morning rondelay—ever since then she'd been waiting, waiting.

The fair sex, she thought bitterly—a misnomer of the first order. Jill Osborne was not fair to flirt so with her husband at the dinner. Just because her husband was Max Carbone, owner of the museum, did that give her privileges with the artists who supplied her husband's museum with works of art? No!

As she watched Roger's strong hands move over the wet clay she thought of him doing the light fantastic with Jill Osborne the night before. Her mind was a grim reaper of angry thoughts. Those raven tresses of Jill Osborne, she thought, those starry orbs of eyes, those shoulders as white as white blankets of snow. She was a spoiled hussy, that's what she was! She had never worked for the staff of life. And now, ever since the new had leaked out about Roger's success, she was trying to steal him from her—shamelessly!

The night before Roger had beat a hasty retreat to his studio as soon as he and Louella had come home from dinner. There he had burned the midnight oil sculpting and by Herculean effort had finished an entire statue by morning. All in all it had been an exciting night what with meeting Jill Osborne and now getting so much work done. If only Louella would stop her endless bickering.

A Murder Told in Two Hundred Clichés

Needless to say, with such an undercurrent of excitement in him he could not seek the comfort of bed. He had not taken to drink and yet he still felt drunk as a lord. Tired and happy he had finished his work bright and early with a sigh of relief.

Then, before Louella had come in he had seated himself in the window seat and began to retrace his steps. Really, he thought, it had come as a bolt from the blue this meeting with Jill Osborne. He tried to stop this feeling of deep attraction, he tried to nip it in the bud. But it was hard. Looking out over the ground of his house, staring at the trees standing like sentinels he tried to forget.

He thought for a while of his old college days, those happy hours in the halls of learning, studying his art in order to create something that would astound the seething mass of humanity, that would—

It was no use, he could only think of the opposite sex of, to be exact, Jill Osborne. Such a lovely creature. She looked as if she were sweet sixteen. He closed his hands together then and Louella had come in.

Now he was working in silence while she sat sniffling on the chair. I will be doomed to disappointment, he thought, each and every new excitement is undone by this sniveling woman. Every chance acquaintance I make whether it be a long-lost friend of a stranger—so long as it was a woman—Louella accuses me of infidelity. If it were not for those dear ones at home, his little ones, Luke and Marie, he would not be among those present in this house. He would be with Jill Osborne. In his mind's eye, he saw her face again.

Louella stared at the embers smoldering on the hearth.

"I'm hungry as a bear," Roger suddenly growled.

"After last evening's repast?" she said brokenly.

"It could not do justice to my appetite," he said, suddenly thinking of how he used to eat in college, in those halycon days in the institution of higher learning.

"No wonder you did not eat," she said, "You had to join in the merry-making so much you hardly ate at all." Her voice grew hard and bitter. "And a good time was had by all," she said.

"May I venture a suggestion," he said acidly. "In my humble opinion you are not, in the least, equal to the occasion. Why don't you leave me to do my work in peace?"

"No sooner said than done," she snapped and was on her feet in a moment.

She stormed to her room. All to soon, she thought, he'd find out he couldn't do without her mothering cares. All too soon will he regret putting our marriage to the acid test. So this is his heartfelt thanks for everything I've done for him. Such cruel words he'd spoken—and in such deadly earnest!

Well then, he was blissfully ignorant of how much he really needed her. He could never survive in this day and age without her. If he thought he could live to a ripe old age without her he was wrong. Indulging egotism was his ruling passion and it would drive him to the last sad rites before he was forty if he did not learn to respect her care of him.

She lay on her bed sobbing and thinking. The younger generation, she thought miserably, even though she was only seven years his senior. But then, to a woman, seven years was a goodly number of years. She had always had the long felt need to make those years vanish.

"Oh Roger, Roger," she thought thinking of their early years together. Roger had been among the fortunate few artists who found a woman both intelligent and wealthy—one who could supply him with affection and free his mind from financial burdens.

It had been all he needed. His work progressed quickly and soon his work was in the public eye. Excitement ran high and when Maxwell Standish, the art critic

A Murder Told in Two Hundred Clichés

of the *Dallas Cattle Breeders Monthly*, a person of consequence in the art world, said that Roger had a promising future, his career was virtually established.

Then it was that Louella was the tower of strength Roger needed. Though he was a huge hulk of a man, a veritable Colossus in the garret, as it were, he was weak and vulnerable to criticism. Louella knew that and she knew she had to take steps to save his spirit, she knew that drastic action was necessary to relieve the situation.

Drastic measures call for drastic demands on the bank book. But Louella did not shirk her duty. She hired a hall and personally set up a one-man show for Roger. She worked very hard and, on one occasion, her self-appointed job became almost an ill-fated mission when her car, a lethal weapon in the best hands, almost became a death car while she was driving to keep an appointment with some plumbers. She escaped with her life only by the narrowest margin.

But the show was a success. A record-breaking crowd declared Roger's show a brilliant performance and actually broke into a round of applause when he appeared nervously to see how things were going. It was a truly spectacular event.

Louella thought of the even after that show. They had been so happy. After a home-cooked dinner, Roger had favored her with a selection on the xylophone. His slight indisposition had vanished when he'd seen how successful his show was and now he knew the day was a red-letter day for him. His professional career was on its way, no longer would he be marooned in a small town where he had met Louella. Everything was wonderful. That night he and Louella were intimate friends again.

I must catch forty winks, she thought abruptly, shunting aside all moody reflections. But angry thoughts would not leave her. He is asleep at his post, he thought, he is not abreast of the times if he thinks he can live without me. In the milling mass of humanity he would be lost without my guarding presence. Her hands tightened willfully.

"Ah, I am stark mad!" Roger had cried in his studio, meanwhile, throwing down a lump of clay. "Stark made to lose my mind over such a raving beauty!"

Really he felt as if he had lost his best friend when Louella left the room angrily, as red as a beet. He looked down at his hands that were as white as snow under the dark clay specks. Jill Osborne is beautiful but dumb—he tried to convince himself of that but he didn't get to first base. Why do my emotions dash madly about, he thought, why does sensible will-power barely eke out an existence in me? I'm fit as a fiddle, he knew, strong as an ox—and yet, th thought of Jill's soft voice makes me weak as a kitten. This strange debility in his mind—it was food for thought.

He stiffened resolution. Am I to be frightened out of my wits by the angry words of a wife green with envy? No! He ignored the memory of her face as it had been the night before at the dinner party. She had watched him dancing with Jill Osborne and had been pale as a ghost, her skin as white as a sheet.

Well, his so-called better half was dead as a doornail, that was all! The realization suddenly dawned on him. I'm through leading a dog's life! He thought angrily.

He felt light as a feather as he hurried down the hall to the bedroom. He went in and slammed the door. She raised up from the bed with a gasp of surprise, paralyzed with fright. In the silence broken only by his heavy breathing you could hear a pin drop. She stared at him, rendered speechless by his appearance.

It is pure and simple, he thought then, I must dispose of her.

"I want to point with pride at my wife," he said, "but I can no longer do that."

A Murder Told in Two Hundred Clichés

She did now answer him. She gaped at him with mute shock.

"I want the finer things in life," he went on. "Existence with the gentle sex spoils that." His voice grew bitter. "I am the proud possessor of a ship of marriage which has been thrown on the rocks by the sea of matrimony."

"Roger," she moaned, staring at is weatherbeaten face.

"Words fail to express my disgust with you," he snarled. "I work like a dog at my sculpturing, I keep my nose to the grindstone but for what! For you? Look at you—you're getting fat as a pig!"

She recoiled from his words and tried to get up. But he moved quickly across the rug and caught her wrists in a viselike grip. She was as quiet as a mouse as they struggled. For a moment she thought she was going to collapse in a dead faint. But then she cried, "Roger, do not!"

"I'm sadder but wiser!" he snarled. "Now let me lull you to sleep with my hands."

The ensuing scene was one of violence. As Roger's hands closed on her throat Louella felt as if she stood on the brow of the hill of life. All the happy years that had been enshrined in her memory were suddenly thrown aside, broken and dead. Those long years of walking in the sunkissed meadows together, those happy moments— but she could not wax sentimental about a murder.

She struggled weakly with him, the memories flowing through her brain at terrific speed. This adds insult to injury she thought and then the blackness came and swept her away.

He stood over her mortal remains, breathing heavily. With might and main, he thought, I have freed myself. The tower of strength has fallen. I have thrown caution to the winds. I will be a hunted man but it is worth it. He thought again of Jill Osborne's face which beggared description.

"Sleep the…sleep of the just," he muttered to his dead wife as he covered her body with the bedspread. Then he straightened up. I must pull myself together, he thought, create some order out of the chaos that is my mind. There is a method in my madness. Now I will have Jill all to myself. I will take the consequences of this moment.

Then he noticed a bottle on the bedside table. And his hands shook as he picked it up and stared at the pills, the white pills.

"The irony of fate!" he cried out.

She had taken sleeping pills and was, even as he strangled her, was dying. It was too much. Truth is stranger than fiction, he thought, it never rains but it pours…

His head slumped on his chest and he murmured brokenly, "The wheels of the gods grint slowly…"